A CHRISTMAS QUICK SKETCH

A SOUTHERN HUMOROUS HOLIDAY CRIME CAPER

A CHERRY TUCKER MYSTERY (PREQUEL)
BOOK 0

LARISSA REINHART

PRAISE FOR LARISSA REINHART

The Finley Goodhart Crime Caper series

"This is as fun a novel as it is moving and at times heart-breaking, never the more so when the final page comes and readers are only left wanting more."

CYNTHIA CHOW, *KING'S RIVER LIFE MAGAZINE* ON THE CUPID CAPER

"Another great mystery by Larissa Reinhart. Con artists, murder, a cast of sinister characters, and some laughs along the way. Loved it."

TERRI L. AUSTIN, AUTHOR OF THE *ROSE STRICKLAND MYSTERIES* ON THE CUPID CAPER

The Maizie Albright Star Detective Series

"Fun characters, a perfect setting, and a mystery that will keep you guessing until the end, this book truly has it all!"

SHANNON VANBERGEN, USA TODAY BESTSELLING AUTHOR OF THE GLOCK GRANNIES MYSTERIES ON 20 CARATS

"Fans of humorous mysteries like Janet Evanovich's Stephanie Plum, and Elle Cosimano's Finlay Donovan should pick up this series. We all need some fun in our reading lives!"

"I loved this very fun romance mystery novel. Five out of five stars."

"I love the characters in this series, they're what keeps me coming back. If you're looking for a fun series that will keep you turning the pages, you've found it here."

"I highly recommend this series and definitely start with Book 1 you won't be sorry!!! Well written characters and a great mystery. I cannot wait to see what happens next!"

"The perfect combination of mystery, romance, and laughs."

"18 Caliber was my first Maizie Albright Star Detective Mystery--I'm hoping it won't be my last. This was a fun read--a fast-paced caper that kept me entertained until the end."

"The mystery and detective cases drive the story, but Larissa Reinhart's characters steal the show every time."

"NC-17 is simply fabulous. Fans of cozy mysteries, southern chick lit, hick lit, crime capers, and humorous mysteries will love it."

"If you love southern settings with plenty of sweet tea and eccentric characters, the meet up of these two heroines is epic."

"Maizie's missteps make each of her successes an absolute joy, and I encourage readers to delve into this lively, funny, and genuinely satisfying series."

"With visually descriptive narrative, humorous quips, witty repartee and a quirky cast of characters, this was a such a fun book to read."

"Larissa writes a delightful book. Suspense, romance, and some funny situations. [Maizie's] a teen star grown up to new possibilities."

"I love Larissa Reinhart's books because they are funny but they also show the big heart of the protagonist."

"Hollywood glitz meets backwoods grit in this fast-paced ride on D-list celeb Maizie Albright's waning star. Sassy, sexy, and fun, 15 Minutes is hours of enjoyment—and a wonderful start to a fun new series from the charmingly Southern-fried Reinhart."

"Maizie Albright is the kind of fresh, fun, and feisty 'star detective' I love spending time with, a kind of Nancy Drew meets Lucy Ricardo. Move over, Janet Evanovich. Reinhart is my new "star mystery writer!"

"Child star and hilarious hot mess Maizie Albright trades Hollywood for the backwoods of Georgia and pure delight ensues. Maizie's my new favorite escape from reality."

The Cherry Tucker Mystery Series

"Anytime artist Cherry Tucker has what she calls a Matlock moment, can investigating a murder be far behind? A Composition in Murder is a rollicking good time."

"This is a winning series that continues to grow stronger and never fails to entertain with laughs, a little snark, and a ton of heart."

"Cherry Tucker is a strong, sassy, Southern sleuth who keeps you on the edge of your seat."

"Because of Cherry's experiences, she knows that —Super Swine notwithstanding—man has always been the most dangerous game, making her the perfect protagonist for this giggle-inducing, down-home fun."

"The perfect blend of funny, intriguing, and sexy! Another must-read masterpiece from the hilarious Cherry Tucker Mystery Series."

"Artist and accidental detective Cherry Tucker goes back to high school and finds plenty of trouble and skeletons...Reinhart's charming, sweet-tea flavored series keeps getting better!"

"Like front-porch lemonade, Reinhart's cast of characters offer a perfect balance of tart and sweet."

"Reinhart manages to braid a complicated plot into a tight and funny tale. The reader grows to love Cherry and her quirky worldview, her sometimes misguided judgment, and the eccentric characters that populate the country of Halo, Georgia. Cozy fans will love this latest Cherry Tucker mystery."

"Reinhart's country-fried mystery is as much fun as a ride on the tilt-a-whirl at a state fair. Readers who like a little small-town charm with their mysteries will enjoy Reinhart's series."

"This mystery keeps you laughing and guessing from the first page to the last. A whole-hearted five stars."

A CHRISTMAS QUICK SKETCH

CONTENTS

The Christmas Quick Sketch

A Cherry Tucker Mystery Prequel

Third Edition

Published by PAST PERFECT PRESS Copyright © 2019 by Larissa Reinhart

ePub ISBN: 978-1-73252-989-2

Past Perfect Press

Original Publication date: Henery Press; 1 edition (December 10, 2013) in "Quick Sketch" in *Heartache Motel, Three Interconnected Mystery Novellas*

Second Publication date: Good Fortune Farm Refuge (November 20, 2018) in *Sleigh Bells and Sleuthing: A Collection of 16 Cozy Mystery Novellas Featuring Female Sleuths* (non-profit fundraiser)

Printed in the United States of America

BOOKS BY LARISSA REINHART

A Cherry Tucker Mystery Series (In Order)

A CHRISTMAS QUICK SKETCH (prequel)

PORTRAIT OF A DEAD GUY

STILL LIFE IN BRUNSWICK STEW

HIJACK IN ABSTRACT

THE VIGILANTE VIGNETTE

DEATH IN PERSPECTIVE

THE BODY IN THE LANDSCAPE

A VIEW TO A CHILL

A COMPOSITION IN MURDER

A MOTHERLODE OF TROUBLE

Audio

PORTRAIT OF A DEAD GUY

STILL LIFE IN BRUNSWICK STEW

HIJACK IN ABSTRACT

DEATH IN PERSPECTIVE

THE BODY IN THE LANDSCAPE

A VIEW TO A CHILL in CRIMES MOST MERRY AND ALBRIGHT

A COMPOSITION IN MURDER

Box Sets

CHERRY TUCKER MYSTERIES 1-3

CHERRY TUCKER MYSTERIES 5-7

Maizie Albright Star Detective Series (In Order)

15 MINUTES

16 MILLIMETERS

NC-17

A VIEW TO A CHILL

17.5 CARTRIDGES IN A PEAR TREE

18 CALIBER

18 1/2 DISGUISES

19 CRIMINALS

20 CARATS

Audio

15 MINUTES

16 MILLIMETERS

NC-17

CRIMES MOST MERRY AND ALBRIGHT

18 CALIBER

18 1/2 DISGUISES

19 CRIMINALS

Box Sets

#WANNABEDETECTIVE, MAIZIE ALBRIGHT 1-3

CRIMES MOST MERRY AND ALBRIGHT

A Finley Goodhart Crime Caper Series

PIG'N A POKE (prequel, short story)

THE CUPID CAPER

THE PONY PREDICAMENT (coming soon!)

THE HEIR AFFAIR (coming soon!)

LARISSA'S GIFT TO YOU!

THE PIG'N A POKE

A Finley Goodhart Crime Caper prequel

When a winter storm traps ex-con Finley at the Pig'N a Poke roadhouse, she finds her criminal past useful in solving a murder.

Free for my VIP Readers!

Join Larissa's VIP Readers group at her website — LarissaReinhart.com — where she shares exclusive content, news, and giveaways. She calls it her big penpal group and loves keeping in touch with her readers in this way. You'll receive *The Pig'N A Poke* as a gift in your first email.

Note: Larissa will not share your email address and you can unsubscribe at any time.

ACKNOWLEDGMENTS

A huge thanks to Tracy Sands for wanting to know what happened with Todd and Cherry in Vegas. Although you still didn't get that story, I hoped this helped feed your imagination! And thank you to your husband, Albert, for explaining the poker world to me.

Also thanks to my Heartache Motel friends, Terri L Austin and LynDee Walker. This story would not exist without you.

And to my family, you always have my eternal gratitude.

*For poker and Elvis lovers everywhere.
Except for the crooked ones. They don't deserve anything but
jail time.*

ONE
ONCE UPON A FEW MONTHS
BEFORE A NOTORIOUS COFFIN
PORTRAIT...

IN THE SETTING DECEMBER SUN, the fluorescent Heartache sign flickered to life, then winked into retirement. Evidently, most of the bulbs had not been replaced since the Heartache Motel's Memphis inception, somewhere between 1962 and 1983, give or take a lost decade. If I squinted, I could see the remnants of the vintage Triple-A insignia, likely ripped off for fear of a libel suit. It didn't give me much hope. But we were here to help a friend. Because of the friend's circumstances, I shouldn't have been surprised by the seediness of our chosen meeting place.

I supposed when you wanted to find low-down, dirty crooks, you had to look for them in their habitat. Which would also be low down and dirty. And the Heartache Motel matched that bill pretty dang well.

"A cross-country trip to Vegas sounds a lot more exciting in theory. Remind me next time not to do it by bus." I dropped my suitcase on the sidewalk and eyed my traveling companion. How the man could survive an eight-hour bus ride and still look like he stepped out of an ad for *Modern Viking Magazine* was one of God's great mysteries.

I had caught my own reflection in the bus window and almost spit Coke from my nose. My sequined "Not An Elf, Just Short" t-shirt had more creases and stains than da Vinci's original sketches. My fair skin felt drier than a Saltine and somewhere between Halo, Georgia, and Memphis, Tennessee, my makeup had disappeared. I will not mention my hair, but eight hours of piped-in air had produced enough static electricity in my blonde filaments that I could possibly solve an energy crisis.

"Baby, I don't know about this place," said Todd McIntosh.

He had shortened my given name, Cherry Tucker, to Baby, sometime after our first date a few months back. I had given up correcting him. Todd was one of those adorable guys who made their dumb stuff seem cute. But as I didn't see our relationship going anywhere except Vegas, I didn't fret.

"The address matches the one Byron gave me," he continued. "But it looks kind of run-down."

"Bill Campbell's thirty-one-year-old thoroughbred is run down." I pointed to the graffiti-tagging decorating the side of the building and the creative use of plywood as window treatments. "This place is plain ol' sleazy. Are you ready for this?"

"Byron's my cousin." Lines worried Todd's angelic features. "I should be asking you that question. It's one thing to take you along to Vegas, but to ask you to stop in Memphis for this sort of thing…"

"Don't you worry, hon'." I patted Todd's bulky bicep. A teensy thrill spiraled through me, but I squashed it. "I'm always ready to square things right. Besides, I think we've got a great plan."

"Yeah." Todd's grin lit the evening sky brighter than the fluorescent motel sign. "I remember some of your great plans from back in the day."

I had known Todd forever and more. In high school, he had wandered the edges of my social circles, a gangly lone wolf who became a poker phenom when no one was looking. I had returned from college and found he had retained his beanpole height but replaced the lankiness with a chiseled six-pack, sculpted shoulders, and a rock hard boo-hiney.

Throw in the fact that he's a drummer with dimples, so when he'd finally asked me out, I RSVP'd with a "Hell, yes." Against my better judgment.

Which I should listen to more often.

We pushed through the retro gold crackled glass doors and into the wood-paneled lobby. *Blue Christmas* warbled through hidden speakers. Tinsel sparkled from flaccid garlands looped around the room. The Heartache's attempt at Christmas cheer hadn't extended into the scent department. An ashtray had a more festive aroma.

"I got us the honeymoon suite," said Todd. "It included the Christmas Elvis show and a bottle of champagne. Isn't that cool?"

I gave him a what-kind-of-girl-do-you-think-I-am look.

Todd shrugged, but couldn't hide his saucy grin.

Not that I didn't trust Todd. However, sometimes my hormones around beautiful men couldn't be trusted. My mother had had the same problem but gave in to the call of her libido. I tried to learn from my mistakes. Namely, a disastrous romance with a man who escaped me by joining the Army.

Seriously, what level of commitment-phobe uses an Afghanistan bunker as an escape from a relationship?

Behind the garland and tinsel-festooned window stood a hard-eyed woman with auburn tresses teased and combed to achieve heights not seen since the 1960s. Like the motel, no updates seemed to have been made with the staff. The fuzzy wig, foundation-caked creases, and flaky blue eyeshadow indicated some kind of odd time warp. A reverse Dorian Gray, as it were. Spotting us, she flashed a lopsided smile from lips drawn with a shaky hand.

"Welcome to the Heartache Motel." The rehearsed speech came with a deep Tennessee drawl that spoke of much time spent with local whiskey and cigarettes. "We're the only Elvis-inspired motel with staff who impersonate the King's entourage. I'm Ann Margaret. How can I help?"

"We've got a reservation under Todd McIntosh," I said. "I guess he booked us a suite."

"Honeymoon suite," corrected Todd.

"Isn't that cute?" She slid an appraising glance over at me, then stopped on Todd's dimpled grin. "Newlyweds? You'll love our *Blue Hawaii* Honeymoon Suite. One dip in the *Love Me Tender* hot tub with a complimentary glass of the *All Shook Up* sparkling wine and you'll be in wedded bliss."

With a wink toward Todd, she put a hand next to her mouth and mimed whispering, "Or let the misses enjoy the hot tub and you can join me in the bar, honey."

"We're on our way to Vegas," said Todd. "Staying two nights because my cousin lives nearby and recommended this place. Thought we'd shake the dirt from our boots and say 'Merry Christmas' to him before getting back on the bus."

"Vegas? Wonderful," rasped Ann Margaret. "You're honeymooning in the King's second home. Although I'm a little surprised by the recommendation. Do we know your cousin?"

"His name's—" began Todd.

"We're not married, nor getting hitched," I interrupted with a fair hint of impatience towards Ann Margaret's obsession with weddings that likely came from a greater irritation with Todd for pushing the honeymoon envelope. "We don't need the honeymoon suite. Any old suite will do. A sofa is what's needed. Todd here is playing in a poker tournament. I'm accompanying him as a personal cheerleader and to make sure he doesn't get lonely spending Christmas away from home. That is it."

"You need to tell the Colonel all about your poker tournament. He's quite the poker connoisseur." She drew her hand in a Vanna White wave toward the bar entrance at the far side of the lobby. "The Colonel tends bar for us in Suspicious Minds."

With the prepared lines I wished I meant, I turned to Todd and placed a hand on his arm. "Now Todd, you are going to play plenty of poker in Vegas. This stopover was meant to be a visit with your cousin. Then there's Graceland and the art museum." I smiled at Ann Margaret. "I'm an artist."

"Exciting," she purred. "An artist and a poker player."

"I'm also a drummer," said Todd.

"Then you'll enjoy our *Blue Christmas* show. One night only. It's at eight o'clock tonight in the Suspicious Minds bar. One of our gals booked the limited showing."

"Awesome," said Todd.

She tapped the keys on her computer. "Sorry, but looks like you used one of those discount sites, so you can't switch rooms." She winked and held out the metal key attached by a chain to a plastic heart. "Who knows? Maybe you'll need a honeymoon suite by the end of your Vegas trip."

"Maybe," said Todd, grabbing the key. "I'm feeling pretty lucky about this trip."

"Honeymoon? Have you lost your ever-loving mind?" I said. "Save up that luck and spend it on your poker tournament."

"One thing poker's taught me, you never know your next hand." An unusually thoughtful gleam sparked Todd's eyes. "I feel like I'm going to get lucky in all sorts of ways this trip."

"I can tell you one way you're not getting lucky and it involves the honeymoon suite."

That took a little holly jolly out of Todd's step, but I believed in showing all my cards when it came to sharing rooms with themed hot tubs and sparkling wine. I'd had my share of that kind of luck with my first love, Luke Harper, although our suite and champagne were a pickup and six-pack. Now I was older and wiser in the ways of sweet-talking men.

Besides, Todd needed to hone his concentration on the task at hand and then the Vegas tournament. If he won big, we'd discuss his luck in other areas.

TWO
THE TRIGGER

"LOOK AT YOU," said Todd. "You look like walking Christmas."

"Thank you." I fiddled with the silk poinsettia necklace I'd made to accompany my viridian green sweater dress with a gold spangle trim. The red cowboy boots were old, but the color fit the theme. "I have always felt that a seasonal wardrobe should be just that."

"I'm feeling all kinds of holiday cheer. This *Blue Hawaii* room is something else."

"Something else, all right." I closed the door to our kitsched-out room decorated with fake palm trees and a round platform bed. "I like the mural, though. You've got to admire a muralist who has the guts to paint Elvis riding an eight-foot wave on a surfboard. In tiny, white shorts. And judging by the shorts, the artist felt enthused by certain parts of Elvis's anatomy."

"I need to get me some of those Elvis shorts," said Todd.

Before I could stop myself, I reflected on the glorious idea of Todd in tiny, white shorts as we sauntered down the graffiti-dappled hallway. We stopped at the elevator. It groaned in protest at the push of the down button. The doors jerked open, revealing an avocado green box covered in even more explicit graffiti, lit by a flickering single fluorescent bulb.

I hesitated. Our previous trip in this elevator made low-rent carnie rides feel safe.

"Byron should be in the bar," Todd said and yanked me into the elevator before the heavy doors slammed shut on my spangled skirt. "Sounds like everything's ready to go on this end."

"We still need to cast our bait," I reminded him, then mumbled a quick prayer that we'd live through another elevator journey.

Having survived another trip on the tiny Tower of Terror, we crossed through the lobby to the bar. The placard for the Suspicious Minds bar advertised several seasonal shows. As Ann Margaret mentioned, the *Blue Christmas* review had top billing tonight.

Todd tapped a happy rhythm against the small of my back as we entered the Suspicious Minds, decorated for Christmas circa 1965. At the leather-topped bar, a tall, slim man with a thin mustache and the McIntosh thick mane of blond hair sat slumped over a mug of beer.

"There he is," said Todd, hurrying toward his cousin. "Byron. Merry Christmas! Man, it's good to see you. You remember Cherry from high school, right?"

"We were in Drama Club together." Byron offered me a sad smile and pumped my hand. "Hey Cherry, how're you doing? Still painting pictures? Last time I saw you was at my wedding, but near the whole town was there. Look at you in that Christmas getup. You always did dress … interesting."

"Long time, no see." I gave Byron a quick hug.

"Thanks for meeting me. I didn't know what else to do."

"We're ready to help," said Todd. "Got it all figured out."

"Shh." Byron cut his eyes toward the bartender. He waited until a waitress passed to sniffle. Loudly. "Y'all make a nice couple. Just like me and Tina did."

"Byron." Todd clasped him on the shoulder with dramatic finesse. "What happened?"

"I'm sorry. It's just so depressing. Tina will be done with me for sure this time." Byron wept on cue. "Today we were supposed to go Christmas shopping for the kids. We were gonna get a tree and a frozen turkey to fry for Christmas dinner. Nothing I like better than standing in my driveway and frying a bird on Christmas day."

I glanced over my shoulder. At the end of the bar, a huddle of waitresses waiting on drinks had stopped to watch us. "Byron, it can't be that bad. You've got another week until Christmas. Tina will forgive you."

He shook his head. "My bonus and our savings. Gone. I just told my boss what happened. Now I've lost my job. I'm such an idiot."

"I think we better have a beer with this story." I glanced at the bartender, rinsing glasses and pretending not to listen to our conversation.

Byron nodded at me. "Yeah, I could use another beer."

Todd flagged the bartender, a large, balding man in a cowboy hat, bolo tie, and tweed jacket.

"Are you the Colonel?" The hat and tie gave him away, but I thought it proper to ask.

He touched his hat. "Y'all staying at the Heartache?"

"Honeymoon suite." Todd grinned and wrapped his arm around my shoulder for a squeeze.

I gave Todd a sharp glance, meaning to cool it with the honeymoon suite stuff, and turned my attention to the aging cowboy. I introduced ourselves and added, "Todd's on his way to Vegas to play in the amateur poker tournament."

"Vegas, huh?" The Colonel glanced down the bar and motioned to one of the waitresses. "Priscilla, come down here and meet these folks."

He turned back to us. "Priscilla performs and books acts for us. She's a crowd favorite. I also know her from making the rounds. She'll want to meet an amateur on his way to Vegas."

"You found an Elvis-loving singer while playing poker? What are the odds?"

"You're in Memphis, honey." The Colonel smiled. "We all love Elvis. And the Heartache is known for their specialized acts. Naturally, Priscilla would hang out here."

"Naturally." I looked sidelong at Byron, but he was too busy staring at Priscilla to notice.

Priscilla turned from her conversation with a customer to eyeball our group. Studying us, she placed a hand on her daisy-scattered bouffant, then brought the other toward her lips to drag on a cigarette before stabbing it out in an ashtray. A white, fringed halter dress exposed a gravity defying amount of no-expense-spared-medically-induced cleavage. The skirt ended mid-thigh, exposing Priscilla's long legs before hiding her knee and calf in white Go-Go boots.

The effect must have been mind-bending to men back in the day. In the dimly lit bar (and particularly with the help of beer goggles), Priscilla still looked amazing. Unlike her Heartache Motel counterparts, time and the elements had been more effectively hidden. Up close, my artist's eye caught the crow's feet, marionette lines and turkey neck that couldn't be smoothed and filled in by Botox and concealer. Guessing by the work she'd done, she easily must have subtracted ten years from her appearance. Give or take a couple of years.

"Lord, I love that dress," I mouthed in prayer, feeling ashamed by my cobbled Christmas creation. The sweater dress did hug my body, but an ironing board showed better curves.

Priscilla caught my stare. "Honey, you could never pull this off. You need something to pour into a dress like this." She fluttered her lashes at Todd. "That's why I look so heavenly. I fill it in all the right places."

Todd beamed in response.

"Baby doll." she drawled and cocked a finger under Todd's chin. "You are all kinds of delicious. What are you doing hanging with these country bumpkins? I book shows when I'm not starring in them. We could have an act that will knock folks dead."

"Never mind that," said the Colonel. "I wanted you to meet our new guests, not book new acts. He's an amateur poker player, not a singer anyway. Now Cherry, what's wrong with the cousin? I saw him crying over his beer."

Byron looked up from his mug. "I got nailed in a poker scam."

"Poker scam or just a bad beat story?" Priscilla curled her lip and moved to leave. "Sorry honey, I've heard that one too many times from the Colonel. He's lost his shirt playing cards more than once."

"Just a minute, I want to hear about this," said the Colonel. "You should, too, Priscilla. If there's a scam running around here, it could affect our games."

"Ann Margaret at the front desk told us you played poker," I said. "But I'm getting the feeling the law doesn't look kindly on gambling in Tennessee."

"That's why we like to go across the river, honey," said the Colonel.

"Or play in establishments not known to the law." Priscilla winked.

"We've got the same problem in Georgia," said Todd.

"I don't know about that being a problem, Todd," I said and turned to his cousin. "Let's hear it, Byron. Was it a scam, or did you just lose your shirt? What happened?"

THREE
THE DOOR CARD

"IT STARTED when I got a call from Mr. Smith with FBN Business Solutions. He was interested in speaking to me about setting up a slew of machines in his office." Byron studied the Colonel. "I sell business supplies. Copiers, paper, phones, computers, desks. Whatever your office needs, I can provide. Even coffee makers."

"Thanks, but not a lot of need for business machines in a bar," he said. "Particularly at the Heartache."

"Well, I was real excited," Byron continued. "This would be a big commission. I've had a paltry year. I got the call last week and drove over to meet Mr. Smith at FBN. Our meeting was scheduled at eleven thirty and because of the long drive, I thought I could take the rest of the day to do some Christmas shopping or visit the track. I wouldn't be expected back at the office."

"Whoa," I said. "Or visit the track?"

Byron's face lit brighter than Rudolph's nose. "Like the Colonel said, across the river in Arkansas, there's a greyhound track with gaming that's real fun. I don't get there much because Tina doesn't approve of gambling."

My mouth zipped into a thin line. I reminded myself this was not the time to judge. Christmas and all.

"What happened at FBN?" asked Todd.

"I made the sale," said Byron. "He wanted near

everything. The office was new. He said they were just setting up. Something about a satellite office."

"What does FBN do?"

"Dunno. I try not to ask too many questions if they're willing to buy stuff," said Byron. "So, we shook hands on the deal. I got out my paperwork when another guy—Bill, I think his name was—pokes his head in Mr. Smith's office and says, 'Hey Smith, you want us to cut you in on the action during lunch?' Then he sees me and gets all embarrassed.

"Well, Mr. Smith gets a little heated with him and says something like, 'Don't bother us. Doing business here. I'm sure Byron doesn't play poker on *his* lunch break.' Bill apologizes and backs out the door. But because I want to make a good impression, I say, 'That's no big deal. I've been known to play a game or two.' Then I compliment Mr. Smith on how nice it is to see a company that lets their employees kick back on their break."

"Dang," said Todd, "If I knew you could play poker on the job, I would've checked into office work a long time ago."

"Me and you both, baby," said Priscilla.

"So what happened, Byron?" I said, anxious to hurry the story along.

"Mr. Smith said he needs to take a call and leaves me alone in the room. I'm sitting there twiddling my thumbs. Well, actually playing Hold 'Em on my phone. It's taking a while. Pretty soon, I've got to use the john. I poke my head out in the hall and don't see anyone. But I hear some guys in the next office, and think, 'I'll just ask them where the gent's is and maybe they'll know what's taking Mr. Smith so long.'"

"Were they playing a little stud in the break room?" At my glance, Priscilla amended, "Seven-Card Stud."

"Actually, Omaha Hold'em," said Byron. "Which turns out, is not my game."

"Obviously, honey," said Priscilla. "Otherwise we wouldn't be hearing this story."

"Don't feel bad," said Todd. "Was it hi/lo?" He groaned at Byron's nod.

"Why'd you play?" I asked.

"Seems that Mr. Smith got an emergency call and had to step out. Forgot about me in the rush. The guys felt bad and invited me to sit in on a hand or two to wait him out. Plus, one guy, Joe, needed a stand-in to make a sales call." Byron sighed and sniffed. "I know I don't play like you, Todd, but I know my way around a table good enough. I figured I could make some extra change for Christmas."

"How many of them were there?" I asked.

"Just five guys, including Joe and Bill. Everything was going great. The play was easy. These guys didn't seem to know what they're doing. I was cleaning house for Joe."

Todd groaned again.

"What?" I said.

Instead of answering me, Todd said to the Colonel. "We're going to need a round of shots with that pitcher of beer."

"That bad?" I said.

As Byron nodded, a tear rolled off his cheek and fell into his empty glass.

"Get on with it, Byron," I said. "What happened?"

"Joe comes back and I show him the stack of chips I won. He tells me I played so well, he'll split the chips with me. The other guys whine to Joe about their bad luck and how good I am."

"Byron," said Todd. "You should know better."

"I figured they don't play much. When they offered to cut me in, I decided to stay. When Joe had returned, he said Mr. Smith called and wouldn't be back. After all, I was planning on driving across the river to do the same thing against semi-pros. It seemed like a good opportunity. And these guys were fun. Nice, too. Until I lost."

"How much did they take you for?" asked Todd.

Byron threw back his shot, polishing it off with a deep slurp of beer. "By the end, I lost my bonus and was in the hole pretty deep. I borrowed against the house. Joe walked me to a bank. I cashed out my savings to pay them back. I didn't want to lose my sales deal with Mr. Smith by looking like a bad sport."

Todd shook his head.

"Todd," exclaimed Byron. "These guys were good. I went from shark to minnow in a few rounds. I couldn't believe it. Never experienced anything like it."

"Hard lesson," I said. "Sounds like you got caught up in the moment. But how did you lose your job?"

"That happened a week ago Wednesday. I figured with the big commission I'd get from FBN's sale, I'd eat crow to my boss and he could front me some money to cover Christmas. I didn't tell Tina, of course. Particularly because I used my wedding ring as collateral for borrowing from the house."

"Those guys let you do that?" I slapped my forehead. "Byron! How could you?"

"I don't know what happened. I just got sucked in. By winning so much, I kept triggering kill hands. The final kill blind is what did me in, but I really thought I had the winning hand."

"Kill blind?" I turned to Todd.

"They were playing on a limit. Byron's wins probably brought the pot ten times or so over the largest bet. It's a way of doubling the stakes, so a player winning on dumb luck doesn't bet on fool hands." Todd turned to Byron. "But I guess you weren't given fool hands?"

"Nope. By the end, we were past double kill blinds. It was like I was on drugs or something. That pile of chips kept growing in front of me. I know I have trouble controlling myself when I get on a roll, but I should have seen it coming." He squeezed his eyes shut and winced.

"Gentlemen players would have stopped you," I said.

Priscilla laughed. "It's money, girl. You think the other players were going to slow down when Byron kept winning?"

"Was he really winning?" said Todd. "I've never seen a game like that."

"Pretty boy, have you played with the big dogs in Memphis?"

"No." Todd's features reddened. "But I think I could tell if someone was cheating. Sounds like collusion to me. Those guys were working together to draw Byron in."

"Dang, Byron." I hugged him. "I'm sure Tina will forgive you if you just fess up."

"Tina pledged to honor me rich or poor, but you think she's going to keep that promise when she finds out what happened?" Byron hung his head. "Tina's going to pack up the kids and move back to Georgia before you can kiss Todd a Happy New Year."

"I'm looking forward to that." Todd wrapped his arm around my waist.

"Never mind us kissing at New Year's," I said, wiggling out of his arm. "What happened with your boss?"

Remember, I had to leave the contract with Mr. Smith because he left for an emergency?"

"Right, an 'emergency.'" I made quote signs with my fingers.

"By Thursday, Mr. Smith hadn't emailed his signature or sent back the contract."

I slapped my forehead. I needed to stop doing that before I gave myself a permanent handprint.

"I tried calling all day Thursday and Friday. Nothing. I'm panicking now because my boss is asking me for that contract every twenty minutes. This week, I drove back to FBN. Nobody's there. The door is locked, so I went to the management office. The building manager said nobody's rented that office in a few months. She showed it to some guy earlier in the week, but not a Mr. Smith, Joe, or a Bill. And definitely no FBN. She finally opened the office to prove it hadn't been rented, and she was right. The office was empty."

"I called my boss, reported it, and he fired me." Byron's face fell into his hands and his shoulders shook. "Then I called the police anonymously. It's illegal to gamble in Tennessee, and I was afraid of getting charged. There's no way to get the money back. And no way to get my wedding ring."

"Oh, Byron." I rubbed his shoulder. "I'm so sorry. You were stupid to play poker, but you were conned by professionals. Nobody could have seen that coming."

Todd grunted and swigged his beer.

"You're that good, sugar?" asked Priscilla. "You think you could have beaten those guys?"

"Don't see that it matters whether I can or not." Todd set his beer down. "Doesn't change things for Byron. Now he's broke. Lost his job, his wedding ring, and his wife. Nearly got arrested. And his kids get no Christmas."

Byron broke into a sob, muffled by his beer mug. Over his head, the Colonel and Priscilla exchanged a look.

I noted that look and wondered if Byron and Todd really knew who they were dealing with. I had a feeling they'd just laid down cards that could easily be trumped.

FOUR

THE ANGLE

"HOW TERRIBLE FOR YOU, BABY." Priscilla laid a hand bedecked in glittering cocktail rings on Byron's forearm. "At Christmas, too."

The Colonel lifted his hat and smoothed his nonexistent hair. "I've got a buddy in Mississippi who told me a similar story. Hit and run games all over the area."

"Any idea who it could be?" I asked.

He shook his head and readjusted his hat.

"We've got to do something," I said. "If not for Byron, for his kids. They're forever going to associate Christmas with their momma, kicking their daddy out of the house."

Much like memories of my own Christmas past when my Momma took off to God Knows Where after my Daddy passed. Leaving me, my sister, and brother to be raised by my grandparents. This year, celebrating Christmas in Vegas had sounded like a wonderful idea.

"I'm desperate here," said Byron. "Todd, you're pretty lucky. You think you could put some money down at the track for me? I'll pay you back when I can."

"I'm better at cards than picking odds," said Todd. "Maybe I could try to win some money for you, though. Colonel, you mentioned y'all play. Do you think you could get me into some games?"

The Colonel pulled a thin cigar from the inside

pocket of his jacket and rolled it between his fingers. He studied Todd for a long moment. "Do you think it's wise to risk your money, son? Don't you need it for your Vegas tourney?"

"I don't think I'll play well in Vegas knowing I didn't try to help out Byron. I don't know any other way to raise money for him."

"I could sell some sketches for you, Byron," I said and noticed no one jumped on that idea. "There's got to be a better idea than gambling your own savings, Todd."

"No one's going to contribute to a GoFundMe for that story, honey." Priscilla rolled her eyes.

"We could help Todd find a game, though," said the Colonel. "What d'ya think, Priscilla?"

"Why not? I'm always looking for a good time." Priscilla shrugged, then fluttered her lashes at Todd. "I'm sure the boys and girls would love to get in on playing an amateur on his way to Vegas."

"Let me make a few calls." The Colonel pointed his cigar at us. "Fact is, Priscilla and I get better odds in the Memphis underground than over in the legal, civilian joints in Arkansas."

Between sips of beer, Todd's gaze flickered over the Colonel. "Actually, I think I can win more money in one game with a large pot limit than trying to hit a bunch of tables in a weekend. Any big games tomorrow?"

"Not sure about that." The Colonel played with his cigar. "Haven't heard of any."

"Can you set up a game?" said Todd. "Maybe y'all know some players with deep pockets who'd like a little risk?"

"I'm game. Might take some quick organizing." The Colonel flicked a glance at Priscilla.

"Alright," drawled Priscilla. "We could talk to some folks. Consider it a Christmas gift to your sorry excuse of a cousin."

"Hey," said Byron.

"D'you think you're good enough to hang with some big dogs?" asked the Colonel. "They'll think it's a dream table."

"I'll do my best," said Todd. "Who knows? Maybe those crooks will show. I can beat them at their own game."

"We can't count on it, but just in case, Byron better hang low so they don't spot him." The Colonel examined the cigar as he rolled between his fingers. "That'd be an interesting development, though. But very risky for you, Todd."

"Sugar, this sounds all kinds of fun," said Priscilla. "We'll split the table charge?"

"No, we give it to Byron to save Christmas," I said hotly. "I suspect everyone involved wants to spread some good will to men during this season? Even gamblers like y'all?"

"Honey, good will to men is my middle name." Priscilla winked, then fluttered her fingers. "Got to go check on my performers. I hope y'all are staying for our Christmas show."

"Let me make some calls." The Colonel slipped the cigar between his lips and trotted toward the back of the bar.

"You were real convincing, Todd. You, too, Byron," I whispered. "I think they went for it."

"I just wish the story weren't true," sighed Byron. "Now that this part is done, I'm going to need more alcohol."

The lights flashed. Across the room, Priscilla announced the floor show. Byron and I turned on our stools. Todd slid off his stool to stand next to me.

"Todd," I said, relaxing into his shoulder. "If you win a lot of money in Vegas, what will you do?"

He twirled my poinsettia necklace around one finger. "Spend it on you, I guess."

"You have the chance to make some serious cash. Do you want to keep driving a delivery truck in Halo?"

"I like Halo," he said. "I don't mind driving a truck. It gives me time for my other pursuits."

"What other pursuits? Poker and drumming?"

"Maybe I'd use the money to buy a mess of paintings. That way I could support your interests."

"Somehow I don't see you as an art collector, but that's sweet of you to say." I snuggled into his arm and enjoyed the feel of his brawny body against my back.

On the small stage, a jowly Seventies-era Elvis in shades, white cape, and Santa suit grabbed the microphone. With a few preliminary hip thrusts for the crowd, he broke into *Blue Christmas*. Behind him, a vertically challenged man in an elf costume made moves evoking the Temptations.

"Would you look at that," said Todd. "An elf who can dance."

"That singer looks real familiar." Byron squinted. "But I'm seeing two of him."

"Byron, that's not really Elvis," I said. "No more Rock-a-Hula cocktails for you."

"I think this plan is going to work just fine." Todd leaned over to kiss me on the cheek, causing a rush of heat to prickle across my skin. "Like Priscilla said, these kinds of hustlers will be interested in playing an out-of-town player. We should reel them in that way. Especially if those con-artists are local like you think."

"The way the Colonel and Priscilla started salivating over the idea, I think they won't even need to throw a wide net. While you work on winning back Byron's money, I'll work on figuring out who the hustlers are."

"Getting rich is the best way to get even."

"Y'all, we need to be careful." Byron's blue eyes snapped from their Rock-A-Hula haze. "Messing with these guys is dangerous, Cherry."

"You're forgetting my grandpa's best friend is the Forks County sheriff. Uncle Will was as much a part of my raising as Grandpa Ed and my Grandma Jo, bless her soul. I picked up plenty of ideas from Uncle Will. Hell, I used to do ride-alongs for kicks."

"We could be walking into a very serious trap. Or get caught by the cops."

"Have some faith. It's Christmas." My confidence was all for show, but as much as for myself than for Byron.

We refocused on the musical performance. As the Elvis-wannabe broke into *Merry Christmas Baby*, the Colonel returned. We turned to face him, leaning into the bar to hear the Colonel.

"The fix is in," said the Colonel. "The game is on. Honey, looks like you were right about gamblers wanting to spread a little Christmas cheer. I've got some names for y'all."

"See Byron?" I smiled and slapped his shoulder. "We'll get you that frozen turkey and find a way to get your wedding ring back."

However, nothing was ever that easy. Even for low-class high rollers, like us.

FIVE

THE ACTION CARD

THINKING it safer to leave Byron in the *Blue Hawaii* suite, Todd and I borrowed Byron's truck to scope out the Memphis late night poker scene. Armed with an address and names from the Colonel, we snagged a map from the front desk and drove into the city.

"Driving here is not much different from driving in Atlanta," said Todd. "But thankfully, the Memphis streets are better marked."

"Speaking of Atlanta," I said, gazing out at the bright city lights. "I think I should call Uncle Will and tell him what's going on."

"Now Cherry, that's not the plan. You're going to get these guys in trouble. They're doing a lot to help us."

"Uncle Will may be a sheriff, but he'll see my reasoning. He's probably got a friend or two out here. Seems like he's networked across the country. At least across the South, anyway."

Todd shook his head. "You bring in law enforcement and the Colonel will fold the game. We're dealing with pros."

"Pros?" I scoffed. "What's the deal with him and Priscilla, you think?"

"What do you mean? Other than working at the Heartache and playing poker together?" Todd looked at me. "Like romantically? She's awfully flirty, but he doesn't seem to care. They're not married. No rings."

"I don't know what I mean." I waved my hand. "I don't know why I care. They both seem kind of sad, don't they? I'd hate to be that old and working in a sleazy dump like the Heartache. What's it all for?"

"Elvis?"

"Maybe they've got too many gambling debts and they're trapped." I shook my finger. "Something to think about Todd."

He pulled into a parking lot off Beale Street. We ambled along the sidewalk, joining the other tourists enjoying the street entertainment. Reaching a corner, Todd checked his handmade map and turned right. We followed the side street several more blocks and watched the neighborhood grow from sketchy to foreboding. Todd grabbed my hand before turning down a road that looked more alley than street. He pointed to a flight of stairs leading to a basement door.

"This must be the Green Room." Todd squeezed my hand and pulled me around to face him. "It's probably better if you just let me do the talking. You're just here to watch. We need to get players interested in a big game, and you've told me a million times how much you don't like poker. We don't want to scare them off."

"I don't like my part of the plan," I said. "I'm more of an action person. Watching is boring."

"I know you are, baby, but you've got to trust me on this." He chuckled nervously and began strumming the side of his leg with his free hand. "It'd be better if we stick to the plan. Remember how you said you'd help? You've got your part, and I've got mine. They're just a little different, is all."

"Fine," I said. "I'll do it to save Christmas for Byron. But in the future, don't expect me to play the 'little woman' role. It makes me itchy, like I want to hit someone."

"That's kind of a turn on." His strumming became a drum roll.

"Don't get weird on me now." Sometimes I couldn't tell if Todd was joking or all foam and no beer. "You better calm down and focus, Mr. Big Shot Poker Player."

"All right." Todd beamed. "Let's go find Fred and this other dude, Luther. The Colonel said they'll help us set up a game."

We followed the stairs to a jade green door. No sign. Not even a light shined over the battered door. The stairs were littered with cigarette butts and gum wrappers.

"I feel like I'm walking into a speakeasy," I said. "Reminds me of Savannah."

We pushed open the heavy door and came face to face with a man the size of a well-proportioned hippo and with a face to match. He sat behind a cage of chicken wire surrounded by shelves of random items.

"Is this a pawnshop?" I asked. "You got any wedding rings in here?"

"No," said Hippo. "And no."

"We're looking for Fred and Luther. The Colonel sent us."

"Barry?" said Hippo. "Go on back." He motioned to a door on our right and pressed a buzzer.

Todd yanked open the door, then blocked the entrance with his body.

"What are you doing?" I stood on my toes, trying to see around him.

"Just checking the place out," whispered Todd. "That big guy makes me nervous. Jeez Louise, look at all those tables."

I pushed on his back. "Let me see."

We entered the basement room set up with a bar and a dozen tables. A string of Christmas lights hung over another barred window that opened onto Hippo's den. Men and a few hard-jawed women briefly shifted their glances our way. Tension vibrated off the players, although none showed much evidence of the pressure.

Behind the bar stood a woman wearing a skintight skirt and a transparent black blouse. A streak of scarlet slashed her jet black pompadour. She crooked her finger at us, and we strolled to the bar.

She scanned my Christmas dress for a hard minute before greeting us. "Are you looking for a game?"

Todd leaned on the bar. "Do I buy chips from you?"

"Do I look like a bank?" she snapped.

"Hold on to your money, Todd. We're looking for Fred and Luther," I said. "We're not interested in playing."

"You don't chat with anybody without playing. This ain't that kind of social club."

"What's the buy-in?" asked Todd.

"Now Todd." I gritted my teeth, preparing for my 'little woman' role. "We can't afford to spend money on cards. You can wait for that big game tomorrow night and then you've got the tournament in Vegas. That's plenty of poker, the way I see it."

"Too bad Blondie holds your leash so tight." The Psychobilly chick raised her eyebrows and pursed her crimson lips. "Big game tomorrow night? Sounds like your plate is full, handsome."

"Yes, ma'am." Todd gave her his best hayseed smile. "I am blessed with the chance to compete in an amateur tournament in Vegas. Tomorrow night is just for fun. The Colonel over at the Heartache Motel is throwing a little game of Hold'em for me. He thought Luther and Fred would be interested in joining. Maybe some of Luther and Fred's friends, if they want to play, too."

Bending forward, he held a hand near his mouth. "But it's a big limit, so only serious players."

She narrowed her eyes. "Where are you gonna hold this little game?"

Todd turned to me. "Baby, where are they holding the game? How'd I miss that part?"

I sighed. "Todd, you've got to start paying attention to details. A new visitor's center at Graceland. The Colonel knows a guard who'll let us use a room."

"That's new construction," said Psychobilly. "It isn't done yet. You must be mistaken, Blondie."

"I'm not mistaken, Alt Girl." I knew her type in art school. "The new construction was the point. It's not like we could use the real visitor's center. The Colonel didn't want to hold it in the usual places. He's worried about cops."

"That so?" She folded her arms on the counter. "Well, I can't let you stay to chat unless you're playing. So if you want to say hello to Fred and Luther, you best buy some chips and sit your butts at a table."

"No problem," said Todd, fishing a twenty from his wallet. "Will this do? What's your name?"

"I'm Lucinda. I can't believe the Colonel is wasting his time with you. Go get your chips from Little Jimmy at the front door. Fred and Luther are at the back table. I'll get them to deal you in next hand."

We left the bar to retrace our steps to Little Jimmy, aka the hippo. I hoped there was no Big Jimmy.

"Todd," I whispered. "Are you sure you can play with these guys?"

He looped an arm around my neck and bent to kiss me on the cheek. "Don't worry. If I lose a little money tonight, it means more money for Byron tomorrow."

"I'm not following your logic. If you lose money tonight, you won't have much to play with tomorrow."

At Little Jimmy's cage, a stumbling negotiation ended with Todd handing over a precious five hundred dollars. We circled the room to the back table where Lucinda stood chatting with the men.

Her surly demeanor had switched to a teasing smirk. "Fred. Luther. This is Blondie and Handsome. The Colonel sent them."

A young, dark-haired man in sunglasses and a baseball cap smiled up at me and held out his hand. "Hey, I'm Fred." Two dimples popped in his cheeks.

"Hey, Fred. I'm Cherry." My heart skipped. I'd never met dimples I didn't like. I swiped my hand against my dress before grasping his.

The lanky, young guy sitting next to him wore a fedora and a shiny suit that might have walked out of Frank Sinatra's closet. He tipped his hat to me. "I'm Luther."

"Hey Luther, nice to meet you." I grasped Luther's hand for a hearty pump. "Y'all seem so young. You were not what I was expecting at all."

Lucinda scowled. "There are your chairs. Deal them in, Fred."

"Don't deal me in. I don't know how to play," I said. "I'll just sit here and chat."

"You don't play, you don't sit," said Lucinda. "You can wait outside or with Little Jimmy."

I turned away from Fred's adorable face and confronted the pin-up knock off. "It's December. I'm not waiting outside."

"Then I guess you go in the cage."

"I'm not sitting in any cage."

"Cherry," said Todd, slipping onto a chair. His fingers strummed the table. "Why don't you sit at the bar? I'm sure that'd be okay, right?"

With long dimples framing a face God normally reserved for angels, the smile Todd gave to Lucinda would have warmed the Grinch's tiny heart.

"Maybe I'll sit in on this hand." She hopped into the chair next to Todd. "Blondie, go watch the bar."

A sudden shot of jealousy blasted through me, but before I said anything, my brain reminded my mouth about my promise to Todd and the reason for this trip to the Green Room. I was here to save Christmas for Byron's children. I could take the high road. I wasn't going to let a Psychobilly femme fatale knock the joy and tidings out of me.

I wandered back to the bar. Sliding onto a stool, I pulled a pad and pencil from my messenger bag. Choosing a guy from the closest table at random, I began to surreptitiously sketch him. My pencil flew over the paper, first roughing out basic features, then circling an oval around the figure, cameo style.

Poker players made excellent models. They barely moved.

After twenty minutes, Luther wandered to the bar and tipped his hat toward me. I flipped the page to an illustration I had mocked up earlier as a decoy.

"What are you doing, doll? Drawing pictures?" He leaned closer. "Say, that's pretty good. Can you do one of me?"

"Sure." I flipped to a blank page. "Did Todd fill you in on the Colonel's game tomorrow?"

"Sounds like a gas." He leaned against the bar with a rocks glass in hand, attempting his best Rat Pack pose. "Heard you're raising money for a family in need."

"You watch a lot of old movies, don't you?" I swept my pencil over the paper, capturing the arc of his shoulder and the swagger in his grin.

"Only the classics, baby doll." He winked.

I ripped the sketch from my pad and handed it to him. "What do you think?"

He gazed at the paper and glanced at me. "That's my mug, all right. Say, you're fast. I bet the other cats would like their picture made, too."

"I worked as a quick sketch artist at Six Flags during high school."

"The fellows and I have been talking. We need a good blind for the visitor's center. We think you'll be just the ticket."

"Ticket for what?"

"Fred knows a guy, who knows a guy. You think you can pretend to paint a wall?"

BLESSING my foresight to carry a box of sharpened Berols, I kept my hand flying over the pages of my sketchpad. I'd planned to show Byron my sketches, hoping he might identify a suspect. But I also figured by selling sketches to players, I might make a few bucks for Byron, too.

When the players weren't looking, faces materialized in my book. As games broke up, players stretched their legs and sauntered to the bar, where I offered to make them a quick sketch. Dropping a twenty on a drawing meant nothing to these big spenders. In my most humble opinion, their egos enjoyed the quality artwork depicting them playing fast and loose with the cards.

Above all else, a portrait artist must feed the vanity of their subject. Either that or lose the commission.

Happily, I zipped off my contribution to the underbelly of illegal gaming. One night's work could buy a tree, turkey, and stocking stuffers for the kids. If Byron were smart, he'd buy Tina something extra nice. Like a girl's weekend to Gatlinburg to forget her troubles.

After Luther had returned to Todd's table, I concentrated on my sketchpad and not on Lucinda's flirting. Or the dwindling pile of chips in front of Todd. I knew nada about poker, other than it required one to sit without moving for long periods of time. As an artist, I found that my greatest encumbrance. That's why I got so good at quick sketching.

When a puff of hot, fetid breath blew down my neck, I jerked around in my seat and found myself squaring eyeballs with Little Jimmy.

"Whatcha doing?" he growled. "We can't allow loafing in here."

"I'm watching the bar for Lucinda while she plays."

"What's with that paper and pencil?"

Little Jimmy's neuron connectors needed some greasing. But perhaps he was not a connoisseur of the art world and had never seen doodling such as mine.

"Quick sketches," I said with even less humility than usual. "Your customers are loving them."

I pointed to a particularly lucrative table where my portraits lay next to the corresponding players.

Oddly, instead of praising my craftiness, Little Jimmy's face turned an interesting shade of puce. Then he tried to snatch my pad.

"What the heck?" I shoved the pad into my messenger bag and jumped off my barstool. "Didn't your momma teach you not to grab?"

"Give me that notebook." Little Jimmy reached past his glacier-sized overhang to snatch my bag.

Lucky for me, I easily out-dodged Jimmy's T-Rex arms. I circled behind the bar to get additional barriers between me and his stumpy range.

"Chet," Little Jimmy called over his shoulder. "This gal's drawing pictures of everyone in the Green Room."

I peeked over the bar. An average looking, middle-aged man jerked his head up at Little Jimmy's holler. I tried to remember if I had sketched Chet, but his blend of ordinariness set him apart from the Green Room's more interesting characters.

With a scowl, Chet tossed some chips into the center of the table and folded his hand. "Dammit, Little Jimmy. Why do I end up doing everything myself?"

"What's the problem?" I said. "Does Little Jimmy expect a cut from my commission?"

My voice carried to Todd, who suddenly blinked out of his poker slump and straightened. Lucinda also turned in her seat, with Luther and Fred following suit. The other guys at the table took the distraction as a chance to relax their features and check their cards.

Chet pushed out of his seat and rose, sharpening his gaze on my half-stoop behind the bar.

I ran for the door, ready to protect our sketchbook lineup of possible suspects. I assumed Todd would come after me. More like I hoped Todd would come after me.

His major character flaw would be his ability to forget about me while playing poker. A pretty big flaw if your girlfriend is about to run out of an illegal gaming room and into the gritty streets of a city she's never visited.

I yanked open the first door and hurled through it. Took three steps past the cage and reached the outer green door.

Behind me, the first door slammed into the wall. Behind me, I could hear Little Jimmy's laboring breath. I was not much into organized exercise, but I had no doubt I could easily beat Little Jimmy.

However, I did not count on Chet. When I grabbed the door handle, Chet grabbed me.

"Hold on there." He spun me around.

My back slammed against the door. I gasped. "What's the problem?"

"I need to see that notebook."

"It's just sketches. I'm an artist."

Chet jerked my satchel off my hip and flipped up the front flap. He pulled out the sketchpad and pushed aside my attempts to snatch it back.

"You can't take my sketch pad," I said. "I'll charge you with robbery. That's an expensive book. I'm going to use it in Vegas."

Chet gave me a hard look and began tearing sheets from the book. Drawing by drawing, one hundred pound superior paper fell to the dirty and damp cement.

"Hey," I cried, fearing Chet or Little Jimmy knew we wanted the sketches to identify the hustlers. "Those are just practice sketches. Your players bought the real drawings."

When the sketchpad was half-empty, Chet glared at me and shoved the book through the hole in the cage. "Little Jimmy, shred it."

I gasped. Turn my luxurious, acid-free, multi-media

paper turned into confetti strips? "If you had asked nicely, I would have given you your portrait for free."

"Get out," Chet said. "I don't ever want to see you or your notebooks in the Green Room again."

"Gladly," I said. "But I'm waiting for someone."

He reached behind my back, jerked the door open, and shoved me through.

My boot heels struck the stair behind me. I teetered and sat down hard on the third step. The heavy door slammed shut.

"Chet," I said. "I have no idea who you are, but you just ticked me off."

SIX

THE SLOWROLL

"WE'VE GOT A BUSY DAY," I said to Todd and Byron
the next morning.

We breakfasted in a diner down the street from the
Heartache. After sharing a room with two men and
their raucous snoring, I needed a stronger brew than the
tepid brown sludge the Heartache tried to pass off as
coffee. Rather than sleep on the padded plywood and
cigarette burned object the Heartache called a sofa, I
used my time re-sketching the Green Room's players
from memory on the motel stationary.

I also made a fair likeness of Chet and Little Jimmy
and emailed them to Uncle Will using the Heartache's
business office. If you can call a closet holding a fax ma-
chine and an ancient Dell, a business office. I'm surprised they didn't have dial-up. In the room, we had to
pay for the internet.

"I don't think I can take another night of sharing a
bed with Byron," grumbled Todd. "This better work.
I'm not taking him to Vegas."

"You're just grumpy because you lost money last
night," I said. "I sure hope it was worth the time with
Lucinda when you could have been watching Chet and
Little Jimmy roughing me up."

Todd wisely kept his eyes on his gravy and mouth
full of biscuit.

"That's a first for you, Todd." Byron laughed. "You never lose."

"I apologized plenty last night." Todd's ears brightened to Rose Madder. "I found out Chet runs the Green Room."

"I'm not asking for another apology, Todd. I'm merely pointing out the facts of last night to Byron. And I must say, Byron, you are lucky to have a cousin so full of holiday cheer that he was willing to lose at poker for an entire hour and forty-five minutes while his girlfriend sat on a cement step outside the Green Room. Freezing her hind end off. Of course, he was distracted by his new friends, Chet, Little Jimmy, and Psychobilly Girl."

"Who the heck is Psycho Bill's girl? You mean Lucinda?" Todd's ear color deepened to Red Medium. "She's fixing to come tonight."

"Then she better learn to keep her hands to herself. That's why you lost. Couldn't concentrate with Lucinda breathing down your neck. Don't think I didn't see her rubbing your leg with those trashy press-on nails."

"Lucinda's pretty good at cards," Todd said to Byron. "Knows a lot of people in Memphis, too. She even met Chris Moneymaker once. Played a round of Omaha with him. What a gal."

That remark almost put me off my ham and egg sandwich, but I was never one to let crushes on tacky girls to interrupt my love for a good biscuit.

My irritation with Todd was somewhat alleviated by the approach of the Colonel and Priscilla. The Colonel still favored his hat and tweed coat, but Priscilla had changed to a studded denim jumpsuit.

I brightened at our complimentary outfits. With the brisk December weather, I also wore studded jeans and a cropped denim jacket. But I'd emblazoned the back of my jacket with a Christmas tree and the back pockets of my jeans with silver and gold ornaments.

Adorning my butt with bling tended to disguise what God had forgotten to contribute.

"Howdy, visitors." The Colonel clenched another unlit cigar in his hand. "How was your visit to the Green Room last night? Are Luther and Fred all set?"

"Yes, sir," said Todd. "They're spreading the word about the game. They also had a good idea on how to get the party into Graceland without causing too much fuss."

"I heard you're gonna paint a wall," said Priscilla, sliding in next to me.

"I have a great idea for that," I said. "I'm going to do a mural and draw a series of Memphis musician pictorials. Unfortunately, my good sketchpad was eaten by Little Jimmy last night. I still have my pencil box, but I'll need more supplies."

"I hope you include me in this mural. Y'all went up early and missed my stage act at Suspicious Minds last night. Even Santa Elvis and his elf congratulated me. The Lord did not stop at good looks when he handed me His blessings."

"I'd be happy to draw you," I said, thinking as grateful as Priscilla was for the Lord's blessings, she seemed to have forgotten that He liked a dose of humility as a thank you gift. "But I'm charging twenty dollars for a sketch. It's for Byron's kids."

"Honey, you should be paying me for the chance to make your pencil happy."

"I don't think my pal Lonnie wants you actually painting or drawing on the visitor center's walls," said Byron.

"Byron is right. Painting is just a screen in case a guard shows," said the Colonel. "Todd, I've got one more place for you to visit. We're driving out to Arkansas this morning. We need to spread some mustard across the line."

"You're taking Todd to Arkansas?" I perked up at

the idea of traveling to another state. "What about me and Byron?"

"Byron's going to Graceland," said the Colonel. "We don't want anybody recognizing him at the tables. Besides, he needs to make sure we're all set for tonight. Word has traveled about the game, but I want to cover all our bases. We're taking Lucinda."

"Lucinda," I gasped. "What do you need Lucinda for?"

"She wanted to go." The Colonel shrugged.

"I don't trust her. She works for Chet and Little Jimmy."

"Chet's just touchy. He's protecting his establishment from the law. What were you thinking, drawing the players? If Memphis Police get a hold of your little sketches, it's not just his business he'll lose. You put everyone playing cards in jeopardy."

"The sketches in the drawing pad Chet destroyed were practice for the quick portraits I made for the players. They paid me for drawing them."

"You'll prove useful tonight, providing us a cover for the game. You need to get your painting things together."

"Getting supplies will take an hour tops."

"Priscilla here will help you with anything you need." He nodded at her. "Fred knows the art shop where you can get supplies. Just remember, we don't need a finished product. Just enough to keep the guards and cops from wondering what's going on in the visitor's center at night."

He shoved the cigar in his mouth. "Come on, Todd and Byron," he drawled through clenched teeth. "Let's get going. Graceland closes at four. We need to park the painting truck in the lot before the gates close."

"See you later, baby. Remember, this is for Tina and their kids." Todd pecked me on the cheek. "I promise I'll win big in Vegas."

"You better win tonight for Byron," I grumbled. "I'll

try to recapture my Christmas spirit, but I still don't think it's fair that I have to stay. I've never been to Arkansas."

"Everyone has a job," said the Colonel. "You're the lookout."

The Colonel seemed to relish his role of Mr. Bossy Pants. I remembered being cast as the lookout as a kid when the boys didn't want me interfering with their games. I didn't like it much then either. However, I'd suck it up for Byron's children and the baby Jesus.

"What about the real workers at Graceland? This isn't like breaking into the Halo High School stadium to drink behind the bleachers. That property belongs to one of the most important figures in American history. According to my Grandma Jo, anyway."

"Graceland is giving the construction workers a few weeks off for the holidays. They're also waiting for some flooring or something or other that's been delayed," said Byron. "We won't see any of those guys."

"'Course if we're caught, we'll be in a hell of a lot of trouble. Yourselves included," said the Colonel, brandishing his cigar at me. "Maybe y'all especially."

"How's that?"

"It's your idea, ain't it? And you're tourists. It's not like you know the local PD."

"I guess what you're saying is, you play cards with a few of Memphis's finest." I folded my arms over my chest. "If we're busted, they'll need a couple of names and you'll give them ours, huh?"

"Well, darlin', it's your game. You've still got to play the hand you're dealt." The Colonel smiled, exposing his teeth. "Todd. Byron. Let's leave the ladies to their breakfast."

I scowled, but scooted off the seat to allow Todd to leave. The Colonel had just confirmed what I feared. These players would sell us out quicker than a hot knife cuts through butter. We couldn't trust anyone.

"I don't see what you're all het up about," drawled

Priscilla after they left. She winked and nudged me. "You get to spend the morning with me. Where's that Christmas spirit you keep going on about?"

"Never mind." The last thing I needed was Priscilla lecturing me on jealousy and my lack of holiday cheer. "Do you know anything about painting murals?"

"Do I look like I know anything about painting murals?" She chuckled. "Honey, the only artistic area where I see us pairing up is in fashion design. I'd love to get my hands on some of these DIY creations of yours and make them look a little less ... DIY. Let's get your painting supplies, then work on your wardrobe."

"What are you saying?" I gasped. "Are you dissing my embellishment skills?"

"Relax. I'm not throwing shade at all your artistic achievements. I'm sure you're an excellent ..." She waved her hand. "Whatever you get paid to do."

"Portrait artist." I glared at her and felt the little studs on my pockets digging into my bony backside. Which didn't help.

"Right. Just like I can heat up the mike like nobody's business, I'm also excellent at choosing my wardrobe and enhancing it for my part on the stage."

"And off the stage, as it seems." I pointed at her ensemble. "Unless you haven't updated your wardrobe since the '60s and '70s?"

"Girl, I'm not that old." She scoffed. "Just old enough to have a real appreciation for the King, not like young 'uns like yourself. I was born on his wedding day and my momma named me Priscilla. But I'm getting off track. Whereas you have an eye for two-dimensional art, I have an eye for the living embodiment of art."

"I don't understand what you're getting at and what it has to do with my fashion style."

"I know how to embellish an outfit and you don't. There you go." She patted my hand. "But don't feel bad.

It might surprise you, but I'm not perfect. I'm not good at everything."

"No," I said sarcastically. "Where do you possibly fall short?"

"Oh…" The tips of her nails played across her chin. "Like poker. Just like you seem to love adding ridiculous doodads to your clothing, I love a hot game of risk. But I'm no Phil Ivey, that's for sure. I learned that the hard way, which is why I'm giving you a Come to Jesus about your fashion choices. I want to help you."

"Thanks anyway, but I like my festive look." I tugged my jacket tighter across my chest. "Anyway, I don't even know who Phil Ivey is."

She shook her head. "Ask your golden boy."

"Is that why you aren't playing poker with them today?"

"No." She smiled. "I can handle the gaming in Arkansas. I'm not going with the boys, because I wanted to spend it with you."

"Are you playing tonight?"

"Not tonight." She shook her head. "This is what I'm saying about knowing my limitations. Unless we're talking strip poker, I ain't about to lose my shirt. The boys coming to this game tonight play rough."

I stared at my plate of biscuit crumbs. Rising fear replaced my ire with Priscilla. "Lord, I hope Todd knows what he's doing."

"He's the bait, girl." Priscilla grinned. "How else do you think they're going to hook the sharks?"

SEVEN

THE CATCH

PRISCILLA and I walked back to the Heartache. On a bench before the front door sat Santa Elvis, smoking the stub of a cigarette. He still wore his dumpy jumpsuit–minus the cape. His shades rested low on his nose, and in the sunlight, he looked even more worse for wear than he appeared on stage.

"I guess he's attached to his character," I said to Priscilla.

She arched a brow and rolled her lip. "I suspect Elvis is dressed for the walk of shame. These women who will do anything for Elvis are so tacky."

I longed to point out Priscilla's irony, but kept my mouth closed.

Santa Elvis flipped his cigarette into the bushes and stretched from his seat.

"Maybe I should get his autograph for my sister Casey," I said. "He was actually pretty good in last night's show. She collects autographs, but they're mostly from the bands who come to the Forks' County Fair."

"This is what I'm saying." Priscilla shook her head. "Lord, put an Elvis wig on a man and the girls lose their minds."

"It's not like that." My face reddened. "The autograph is for Casey."

"You think I haven't heard that one before?"

Before Priscilla could antagonize me with Elvis groupie comments, I strode up to him.

"Elvis," I called. "Can I get an autograph?"

He stopped, squinted through his glasses, and mumbled something about paper.

"Unfortunately, my paper was pillaged. I do have a Sharpie." I dug in my bag and fished out a Dixie Cake wrapper. "You think you can write on this? It's only got a little chocolate stuck on it."

He took my Sharpie, jotted on the paper, and slapped it into my palm. Shooting me with his finger, he raised his lip.

"Thanks, Elvis." I knew he was possibly the lamest Elvis in creation, but I had enough of Grandma Jo's DNA to get a teensy thrill from the autograph. Even if it was for Casey.

With a mumbled, "Catch you later, sugar," Elvis strolled to the curb.

Priscilla sidled up to me with an amused snort. "Did Santa Elvis write anything interesting?"

"'Thanks for the rockin' night. Sorry about your TV. Love ya, girl.'" I wrinkled my nose. "Ew. He has me mixed up with another Heartache guest. I feel like I need another shower."

"If there are two guests who look like you, this really is one sorry motel."

A white panel van pulled alongside the curb. Santa Elvis yanked on the passenger door handle. The door popped open, revealing the Blue Christmas Review elf.

The elf had lost his green jingle bell suit and gained a Grizzlies hoodie, jeans, and sunglasses. After a few curt remarks, the angry elf motioned for Elvis to take the back seat.

I leaned toward Priscilla. "I think the elf's not thrilled with Elvis spending the night at the Heartache."

"That's the kind of thing that breaks up bands."

Elvis and the angry elf jabbered at each other for half

a minute. The driver leaned over and jerked his thumb toward the backseat. Santa Elvis offered the elf a choice finger and climbed into the rear.

"I'll be damned if that isn't Little Jimmy," I said. "What's he doing driving around the floor show?"

"Who knows? Maybe Little Jimmy's got a taxi service as a side job."

"I don't like this. That man ruined a perfectly good sketchbook." I glanced at Priscilla. "Didn't you book their act?"

"Elvis is local." Priscilla sighed, making her boredom evident. "He and his buddy do the Christmas review every year. Come on, let's go up to your room. I want to start with that dress you were wearing yesterday. Less is more when it comes to gold trim."

"I'll catch up with you later." I glanced around for a cab. I wasn't sure if I could trust Priscilla, but I needed to follow that van. No time to ask her if I could hitch a ride.

"Where are you going? We're supposed to get your art supplies."

"I'm the one with the beef with Little Jimmy, not you."

"If you're following Elvis, I'm following Elvis, too. I'm not a fan of cops, but I've always wanted to play a detective. I'm often told I look like Angie Dickinson. She wasn't a natural blonde, you know. If only this motel did Frank Sinatara." She sighed. "Maybe I should go to Vegas with you and restart my career."

I felt my breakfast crawl up my throat.

Hooting, she clapped her hands. "No, I've got it. In this getup, I could do *Charlie's Angels*. I'm Jill." She gave me a once over. "I don't see you as Kelly or Kris. You're going to have to be Sabrina."

"Priscilla," I said through gritted teeth. "You're making it real hard to maintain my high standard of gracious Southern charm."

The van pulled away from the curb. Ignoring

Priscilla, I ran toward a yellow cab. She stayed close on my heels. I pounded on the taxi door. The driver sputtered awake and rolled down the window.

"See that white van over there?" I pointed. "Waiting to pull into traffic?"

The driver nodded.

"If you're coming, get in." I shoved Priscilla into the backseat, slid in after her, and scooted forward to speak to the driver. "Follow that van. But don't let it know we're following."

The cab pulled away from the Heartache. We slid forward in our seats, keeping an eye on the van.

"You know, you sound just like the Colonel—ordering people around and making decisions for everyone." Priscilla scooted to the far side of the cab, making a big deal of smoothing the fur collar on her jacket.

"I told you, you didn't have to come."

"I'm not going to miss this performance. It has *Double Trouble* written all over it. One of my favorite Elvis films, by the way."

"Not everything is an act. Byron's family is really in trouble."

"By his own making."

"If you're not sympathetic, why are you doing this? Don't you have better things to do with your time?"

"Sure I do." Priscilla dropped her eyes to examine her manicure, then looked up at me. "But not quite as fun as this."

"Just keep in mind, I'm not doing this for fun. Visiting the art museum would have been fun."

"You're pretty boring when you're not doing the super sleuth act, honey." When I rolled my eyes, she elbowed me. "I think you do find this fun. You just pretend like you don't."

Little Jimmy took the exit for the interstate. Instead of turning northwest toward downtown Memphis, the SUV headed on the ramp leading east. We passed exits for various suburbs. I watched the money counter on the digital meter flip into the ouch zone.

"Holy crap," I said. "If they don't stop somewhere soon, I'm going to run out of money."

The cabbie darted a look into his rearview mirror and caught my eye.

"If you think you can pull over on the side of the interstate, just forget it. This money was supposed to go toward a tree, turkey, and Christmas presents for some children whose daddy just lost his job."

"If you don't pay my fare," said the cabbie. "My kids'll have a daddy who lost his job at Christmas."

Priscilla hooted.

It looked like I was saving Christmas for all kinds of children this year. "Where are we going? Mississippi?"

The driver shrugged.

As the fare inched closer to my breaking point, the van took the off ramp. Our driver slowed and followed, winding through the streets of an industrial area. The van continued over a weedy set of railroad tracks and down a street lined with pawnshops and gas stations offering check cashing services. Young men in hoodies huddled together on corners and watched our cab pass. An honest-to-God hooker waved at us.

I waved back and got an eyeball full of something I'd rather never see again.

As our drive deepened into sketchier territory, Priscilla's eyes grew wider. I took to gnawing on my Fa-La-La-Lavender nails and thought about guardian angels who rescued well-meaning folks from railroad bridges at Christmas.

Finally, the van pulled into the parking lot of a strip mall. I directed our cab to park across the street between a discount furniture and a dollar store. The more familiar surroundings of bargain-priced shops gave me the shot of confidence I needed.

The cab driver pushed a button and the fare counter

blinked. "That'll be eighty-nine dollars," said our cabbie.

I handed over a wad of twenties. He didn't offer change. "Can you wait here? We're gonna need a ride back."

He eyed the Christmas shopping clientele at the discount store. A child pointed a toy semi-automatic at the cab and mouthed "boom."

"I don't know," he said. "I'll give you ten minutes. Then I'm headed back, fare or no."

"Deal. Ten minutes."

I slid out of the cab and hurried to the side of the highway. Semi-trucks roared past and beater cars moved at a slower gait. I heard the slam of the cab door and the patter of plum platforms on concrete. I didn't bother to turn around. Either Priscilla hadn't given up her tail on me, or she really did enjoy my company. Maybe she didn't get many offers to play her favorite character in *Double Trouble*.

At her age, I wouldn't think so.

"What were you thinking, getting out of the cab?" Priscilla looked around and shivered. "This is no place for a girl like me."

"You followed me, remember?"

"Now what, Miss Hicksville?"

"Now I'm just going to jog across this highway and figure out what Little Jimmy, the elf, and Santa Elvis are doing here."

The wind whipped up, as it usually does in the nastier parts of town. Bits of debris and garbage eddied around our feet. A flatbed truck drove by, kicking more flotsam into the air.

"My Sergio Rossi platforms are getting dirty," she whined. "And I'm getting pink stuff stuck in the faux fur collar of my genuine imitation 1974 Bis & Beau original."

"I think that's insulation." I said. "At least you're

warm. I'm freezing. I packed for basking in the Las Vegas sun, not playing Frogger in Memphis."

Noting a break in the traffic, I grabbed her hand and darted onto the highway. A Ford F-250 barreled toward us. In the opposite lane, a Mack truck roared past. Priscilla broke away from my grip and galloped across the remaining blacktop. I chugged my little legs and worked my arms to keep up.

Across the highway, I collapsed against her. "Dang, you're fast. How do you run in those shoes?"

"Honey, getting splattered by a truck is not the way to stop traffic." She patted her hair with her fingers. "My do's a mess. I need a touch up. Let's get this gig done so I can freshen up."

We scurried into the parking lot with our knees bent, backs bowed, and heads up. I imagined our act caught a few snickers at the nearby pawn shop. We hunkered behind the van and peered around the side.

"That door says it's a realty office," I said. "What kind of realtor would want an office in this part of town?"

Priscilla shrugged. "Got to be cheap land around here."

"But who wants to buy it?"

A diner with barred windows and an office for storage units anchored the stretch of businesses. As we pondered our next move, Little Jimmy waddled from the office and clambered into the van.

We dropped to the ground.

"What're we gonna do now?" whispered Priscilla. "Besides, get run over?"

I cut my eyes to the restaurant. "Keep as low to the ground as possible and run for the diner. Maybe Little Jimmy won't notice us."

"Maybe not, but Santa Elvis will."

I peered around the side of the van. Santa Elvis stood in the open realty doorway, lighting up a smoke.

His pose gave him an excellent view of our fine circumstances.

"Crap." I glanced at Priscilla. "I don't see a camera, but this van might have a back-up sensor. As soon as Little Jimmy puts it in reverse, he's going to know we're here."

The engine turned over. I jumped. Exhaust shot out beneath my arm.

Santa Elvis held up a hand and beckoned. Little Jimmy opened his door. The chassis shook as he stepped out of the van. He lumbered toward Santa Elvis, leaving the van running.

I tried the rear door handle, then opened the door. The back of the van held a rack of Elvis costumes, a sound mixing board, and speakers.

"Quick," I whispered and climbed inside.

"You can't be serious," Priscilla hissed. "You might fit in there, but I can't. Haven't you noticed my gams? I'm like twice your height."

"Then stroll back to the taxi and hope Elvis doesn't spot you skipping out behind his ride."

After an effective eye roll, she slid onto the vehicle's floor.

I pulled the door shut and felt the truck rock as Little Jimmy climbed in. *If I Get Home on Christmas Day* blared from hidden woofers.

"Why am I doing this?" whispered Priscilla. She lay bent in a position that would make a frightening crime scene outline. "Bite my tongue, but I am way too old for this."

I curled up next to her. "Don't worry. I told you I'd get us out of here."

"Getting us out is going to require a historic unfold and fluff." She grunted as my bony elbow struck soft tissue. "Start thinking, Shorty. I do pilates, but my joints might not survive this ride."

I nodded, trying to appear confident. But it wasn't her joints I worried about surviving the ride.

EIGHT
THE IDIOT END

AFTER TWENTY MINUTES on the road, I had worked a few ideas through my head for getting out of this van without Little Jimmy spotting us. Luckily, his personal Christmas concert was loud enough that any rustling or mutterings from the back of the van didn't reach his ears.

Good thing, too, for Priscilla had no church mouse qualities. Her sass just about matched my own. She certainly didn't look or act like her contemporaries I knew growing up in Halo. Nor even the other ridden-hard-and-put-away-wet Heartache employees. However, Priscilla was no spring chicken. Scrunched up beside her, I'd gotten an up close and personal look at her parts that hadn't been enhanced by makeup, chemicals, or silicone.

At her age, I wondered if her bravado was an act. Or was she like me? Despite our dire circumstances, adrenaline coursed through me, sharpening my wits. Seeking justice stirred up some kind of chemical slush within me. It juiced me up and revved my motor, giving me a better high than a Red Bull.

However, no matter which way I looked at it, I'd gotten Priscilla into one of my scrapes. Grandma Jo would have tanned my hide. How many times had she lectured me on respecting my elders? Not to mention reacting without considering the consequences. And here I'd gone and combined those two flaws.

I had to get us out of this mess. Quickly.

The van had slowed from its former interstate cruising speed and the engine downshifted into a crawl. The steady dinking of the turn signal caught my ear despite Little Jimmy's Christmas warbling.

"He's getting ready to pull in somewhere," I muttered. "Get prepared."

"Prepared for what?" Priscilla whispered.

"To get out, obviously." I risked a pop up looksee through the back window and fell back on top of Priscilla. "I think we're back in Memphis. Little Jimmy's taking a lunch break. He's pulling into some hamburger place. Dixie Queen."

"Oh, I love the Dixie Queen," said Priscilla. "Haven't been there since I was a child. They have the best burgers and fries. And their freezes, Lord almighty. Not too icy, not too liquidy. Dixie Queen makes them just right. If I wasn't always watching my figure, I'd love an orange freeze."

My stomach sputtered into high alert.

Beneath me, Priscilla cringed. "What's wrong with this van? I think the engine's going to blow. Oh wait, is that you?"

"Hush, he's pulling into the drive-thru. When he stops, we're getting out."

Little Jimmy turned down the music and braked in the drive-thru lane. I grasped the release handle and pulled. The back door flew open. Priscilla and I spilled out onto the asphalt. I scrambled behind the nearby holly bushes, dragging Priscilla behind me. Reaching a Dumpster, we moved behind it, then peered around to check the van.

Little Jimmy had turned around in his seat and still stared openmouthed at his rear door.

"Poor Little Jimmy, let's hope that didn't give him a heart attack," said Priscilla. "He's going to think his van is haunted by the Ghost of Christmas Elvis, wanting his music back."

AFTER I FILLED up on a bacon cheeseburger and a purple cow milkshake, we caught another taxi back to the Heartache.

In the Suspicious Minds Bar, Todd and Byron occupied stools. The Colonel held court as bartender. As Priscilla and I traipsed across the beer and tequila stained carpet, they caught sight of us. Byron choked on his beer. Todd forgot to shut his mouth. Priscilla took the double takes none too kindly.

"Honey, I've shed a ton of Swarovski crystals, my hair is unbalanced, and I lost an acrylic tip," said Priscilla. "Never send me alone with this child again. I'm going to the little girl's room to freshen up."

"Did you get into a fight at the art shop?" asked the Colonel. "Priscilla's limping."

"She's still a little jacked up. She says it's not an arthritis thing and got a little huffy about my mention, so don't bring it up," I said. "We never made it to the art store. However, it's been an interesting morning. I saw parts of the country I hope never to see again. Except for the Dixie Queen, which I would visit every day if I lived here."

The Colonel served me an eye roll that I did not appreciate, so I turned toward the man who never found my statements eye-rolling worthy.

"Hey baby," Todd said, once again forgetting I had a given name. "Did y'all have fun?"

I pondered that question for a few and waited until the Colonel was pouring a drink for a customer. "I wouldn't exactly call it fun. More like a fact-finding mission," I whispered. "I learned that Little Jimmy knows Santa Elvis and the Angry Elf from the Heartache's *Blue Christmas* show. They like to hang out in real estate offices in dicey parts of town."

"Cool," said Todd and elbowed Byron. "Told you Cherry was good at figuring stuff out."

"What do you think it means?" said Byron.

"I don't trust Little Jimmy. We already know he's involved in the underground poker scene. The elf and Santa Elvis might be, too. Either that or it's one odd coincidence."

I cut short our conversation as Priscilla entered the bar, checking her phone. She tucked the phone into her purse and scooted onto a bar stool next to us.

"I didn't have such good luck today," said Todd. "I lost a bunch of money at the tables in Arkansas."

"What the hell, Todd," I said. "I thought you were good at poker. How did you end up getting in a Vegas tournament when you can't even beat these Memphis losers?"

"Watch your mouth now," said Priscilla. "This isn't some hayseed town like where y'all are from."

"How are we going to save Byron's Christmas if Todd can't win tonight? I spent my day in the back of a van, wrapped around an old–"

"Watch your mouth," snapped Priscilla. "I'm the one that got the short end of the stick in that van. Age may only be a number, but my hips and back would argue that point today."

"Well, this has been a horrible vacation. I could have been at an art museum or touring Graceland and not sneaking all over Memphis. A guy named Little Jimmy stuck my best sketchpad in a paper shredder. I spent all my sketching money on taxis and the Dixie Queen. And now Byron's kids' Christmas memories will be of their momma taking the cast iron to their daddy."

Byron rubbed the back of his head and winced.

"Todd, you have to play better tonight," I begged.

Todd circled his arms around me and pressed me to his chest, probably more to smother my hollering than in affection. He smoothed my hair and set a kiss on top of my head. "It's going to be alright, baby. These nice people here are going to help us win Byron's money back. We're going to work together. Don't you worry about a thing."

I turned away from Todd and eyed the Colonel. "I'm counting on you to make this work."

"Then I advise you to stop following Elvis and focus on your part." The Colonel drew a cigar from his pocket and rolled it between his fingers. "We still need those art supplies. Our guy at Graceland has a work order written up. We need to pick it up and set up your scene before four o'clock. You're the cover, so you've got to be inside before the players."

"I'll take you to the art shop," said Todd. "Byron, are you coming?"

He shook his head. "I'm catching a ride with the Colonel."

"Be at Graceland by four," said the Colonel. "Jupiter is Fred's buddy who works at the Art Shop."

"Jupiter?" I said. "Like I need more space cadets in my life."

NINE

THE ONE-EYED JACK

TODD HUMMED "SANTA, Bring My Baby Back (To Me)" while strumming the steering wheel of Byron's F-150. Almost as if he'd forgotten he was bait in a poker game that attracted every skeezy pro in the tristate Memphis area. And he couldn't seem to win a game to save his life. Which was very odd considering his reputation as a poker shark in Halo.

With a population of three thousand.

Maybe not so odd.

While Todd hummed, I picked the Fa-la-la Lavender off my nails. Then sat on my hands to stop myself from eating my cuticles. I had participated in some unbrilliant activities in my twenty-something years, but never had I purposefully committed acts of breaking and entering, vandalism, illegal gambling, and intent to commit a felony.

Well, at least not all in one night. Besides, my nefarious activities were done at home, under the jurisdiction of my uncle, the sheriff.

I needed Todd to share in my jitters. "How can you be so relaxed when we're about to commit a number of illegal acts that might result in losing every penny attached to our names and getting thrown in an out-of-state pokey? Thereby ruining Christmas for not just Byron's family, but ourselves as well."

"I'm not worried."

I knew Todd lived in the moment, but moments such as these were the kind that gave ulcers. "I don't trust these Memphis players. They look like they want to eat you for breakfast."

"It's all good, baby."

"Tell me what happened today besides losing at cards."

"We drove to Arkansas. Went to a gaming room at a track. The Colonel introduced me to a bunch of dudes. We played poker. I lost."

"How'd Lucinda do?"

"She won a couple hands. Then she just kind of hung around. Brought me drinks and a sandwich." He glanced at me with blue doe's eyes I found suspiciously too doe-like. "You said you were with Priscilla in the back of Little Jimmy's van? Now that sounds fun. I like those risky moves you do."

The mention of Little Jimmy's van jogged my memory. I pulled my hands from under my butt to grab Todd's arm. "Priscilla and I never checked out that realty office. I kept an eye on the roads when we were in the taxi. I think I can find it. We could slip over there before we head to the art shop. Hour round trip tops."

"I'd love to, baby, but we can't be late for Graceland. The Colonel said so." Todd's strumming had turned to rapid-fire tapping.

"I promise I won't waste time in the art shop. I'll just grab the supplies we need and leave. Let's scoot over to that real estate office and see if we can learn anything."

I had remembered the exit by the giant ribs sign that appeared just before the interstate off ramp. After that, it was a piece of cake. Follow the road until the pawn shops almost outnumbered the check-cashing shops. Hang a left across from the dollar store. Todd's eyes grew wider the further we traveled into the heart of the industrial jungle.

Only one vehicle had parked in front of the strip

mall holding the realty office. It was not the white van, thankfully. I could not handle hearing Little Jimmy's rendition of "Silent Night" again. He was not a tenor and had no falsetto, no matter his aspirations.

"You didn't go inside?" asked Todd, parking before the office.

"Didn't get a chance," I said. "Little Jimmy just dropped off Elvis and the elf. I wonder where they went."

We approached the glass door.

"Venture Realty," read Todd. He yanked on the door handle. Finding it locked, we smashed our faces and shielded our eyes against the dirty glass to see inside.

Venture Realty had seen better days. Possibly in 1975. The dingy, wood-paneled office had maps tacked on the wall. A TV tray held a massive glass ashtray overflowing with cigarette butts. An actual rotary phone sat on a desk. Next to the desk was an old metal safe with a combination dial that looked like something leftover from a 1930s gangster movie.

"I can see why they don't need bars on their windows like the Cash-N-Carry."

Todd hooked an arm around my waist. "This reminds me of my grandma's house."

"Can you see what's on those maps? Looks like states."

We squinted at the far wall. I could feel the grime transferring to my nose.

"Six of them," said Todd. "Tennessee's got the most pins."

"The others must be the surrounding states," I said, recognizing Alabama. "Most of the pins are near the border of Tennessee."

I held my phone to the door and took a dirt-filtered shot of the maps. "Let's check out the rest of the block. Maybe someone in one of the other shops has information about Venture Realty. But first, smile pretty."

I held up my phone and on cue, Todd struck a pose before the Venture Realty door.

"What was that for?" he asked.

"Memories." I forwarded the pictures to Uncle Will. Shoving the phone into my back pocket, I took Todd's hand, and we ambled down the sidewalk. I breathed a sigh of relief at the diner's closed sign. There's nothing more depressing than an unloved diner.

At the warehouse office door, Todd peered into the high, single window, then jumped back.

"What is it? Storage for body parts or something?"

"No. I just recognized the guy working the desk."

"Who was it?"

"Fred's buddy from the Green Room."

"Let me see." Todd grasped my waist and hoisted me so I could peer into the tiny window. I remembered sketching the man's likeness. "Set me down, please."

For a long moment, we stared at each other. Todd's hands remained wrapped around my waist. Mine laid on his shoulders. More for a convenient resting place than for a romantic interlude. I could tell Todd's thoughts were similarly occupied as his hands were busy pounding the *Bossa Nova Baby* rhythm on my behind.

"Now what's Luther doing working at a storage warehouse in this part of town?" I said, wriggling under Todd's tempo. "I thought he was a musician or something."

"You want to go in and ask him?" asked Todd, stilling his hands.

"Is he coming to the game tonight?"

"Think so."

"In that case, maybe it's best for him not to know that we know his East Bumcrack location."

Todd nodded.

"I don't like this. Chet and Little Jimmy at the Green Room got all worked up about my sketches of players. Little Jimmy leaves Santa Elvis and his crazy elf at this

Venture Realty, but nobody's home. And now we find another poker player, Luther, conveniently working next to Venture Realty."

Todd's attention had drifted from my monologue and into the parking lot.

"Todd, are you with me? This seems real fishy. Can we trust these guys to not screw us over? What if we get busted and they turn us into the cops? How are you going to know who's in your corner when you're playing tonight?"

His gaze snapped back to mine. "Baby, the only one I need in my corner is you."

I blew out a big breath but gave him a hug for being sweet. Judging by the happy rhythm dancing across my butt, Todd had appreciated the hug. However, our corner was looking a little empty.

Or a little too full of people I didn't trust.

THE "ART SHOP" turned out to be The Art Shop, a cement block garage providing custom car paint jobs. The Art Shop specialized in pinstriping, scroll-work, and assorted Grim Reapers. We learned it also had a backroom popular for poker regulars when it wasn't used as a store room.

The Art Shop proprietor, Jupiter, had one glass eye and one Cad Red eye from a constant exposure to paint fumes and energy drinks. Jupiter also blinked incessantly, a handy condition for poker according to Todd. For those playing against him, that tic was more irritant than a tell.

"How am I going to use these supplies?" I said to Jupiter.

We stood in the back room of the garage housing his desk and wire racks of urethane paint in a variety of colors.

I picked up a can of primer and waved it at him.

"Any guard or cop is going to see I should be air-brushing a Camaro and not painting a wall."

Jupiter fixed his eye on me. "I've got kit bottles for mixing. It's all for show, ain't it? You think they're going to look that closely?"

"Cops aren't stupid."

"Got brushes, too. We use them for detail work. Even got your sketch work stuff. We've got to draw up the design on paper before we do it on the car."

Jupiter reached into his desk drawer and pulled out a Strathmore palette pad and a box of Staedtler colored pencils. He tossed them to me.

I caught them, hugging the supplies to my chest. My fingers itched to rub the paper and guess the weight, but I didn't want to appear greedy. "I did lose an excellent drawing pad to the maniacs in the Green Room."

"Keep it."

Todd patted my head at my eager smile. We followed Jupiter out of the office and into the auto bay. While Jupiter walked through the garage, stashing tarps and painter's tape into a garbage bag, Todd and I traipsed toward a Chrysler 300 covered in craft paper and tape. A young guy in a t-shirt, ripped jeans, and skull cap squatted before the driver's door. With a steady hand, he added shading to a trompe l'oeil *Aliens*'s head popping out of the car door.

"Cool," said Todd. "Just like that alien ripped out of that dude's stomach in the movie. Except on a car."

Fascinated, I squatted next to the artist to check out his palette of premixed jars in various metallics. His steady hand gripped a dagger shaped brush with a bat-shaped handle, thicker than I used. The flexible, slanted bristles held the thin line of paint as the artist rotated the brush under the alien's chin.

"Is that a sable brush?" I asked.

He continued his steady progress outlining the alien's bulbous head. "Squirrel."

"Squirrel hair brush with a round hand grip." I

jumped to my feet and turned to Jupiter, my new best friend. "Can I get some of those brushes?"

"The Colonel said to set you up with whatever you need." He motioned toward a rolling, metal tool cabinet. "You aren't really going to be painting, though, right? Just for show?"

"Sure," I said, making my voice sound like I meant it. "Whatever the Colonel says."

I dug into the tool cabinet, opening drawers and running my hands over the smooth wood handles and soft, dark bristles. I didn't plan to stand in a room all night pretending to paint. Any guard worth his tin badge would wonder what the hell I was doing and kick me out if they didn't see any work up on the wall. Despite the Colonel's objection, I still planned to make my mural. I had great skill in cleaning out brushes, so I wasn't going to worry Jupiter with the details either.

Jupiter turned his eye to Todd. "Heard about the game. You're trying to raise money for your cousin who lost his job?"

"Yeah," said Todd, without turning around. He remained stooped over the car, fixated on the emerging alien. "I'm going to give him the house cut. I don't want to see his family suffer at Christmas."

"On your way to Vegas, too?"

"I won a spot in an amateur tournament. The VIP pass to the Tropicana."

"I'll see you tonight."

"Sure," said Todd. "It's going to be fun."

I looked up from the tool cabinet, fumbling the clutch of brushes I held. Todd continued watching the artist and his alien project. However, I stood in Jupiter's nonexistent left periphery and caught his cyclopean examination of the dumb, blond poker bait named Todd.

Jupiter's calculating smile reminded me of my Grandpa's. Just before he carved the turkey on Christmas day.

TEN

THE DARK TUNNEL BLUFF

JUST BEFORE FOUR, we snagged Priscilla from Suspicious Minds, then drove past the famous music gates of Graceland. Something my Grandma Jo would never have forgiven me for not visiting. I imagined her taking a few rolls in her casket over that.

Todd took a tight right off of Elvis Presley Boulevard, following the Colonel's directions to the construction site for the new visitor's center. At the temporary gate, an aged gorilla in a blue security uniform stopped us. He had various tags clipped and hanging on his person and seemed particularly proud of that fact.

From the bench seat behind us, Priscilla muttered something about mall cops.

Before the guard approached, I turned around and fixed her with a lethal stare. "Now Priscilla, you keep still. You're in the back for a reason. Even with those coveralls, your hair and makeup don't really fit the part. Do you think that guard is going to mistake you for a painter?"

"Lord, I hope not." She winked. "I wouldn't want to get confused with the likes of you."

"I'll take the insult in exchange for your hushed mouth."

She gave me the locked lips sign. Todd rolled down the window.

The guard ambled forward, adjusted his cop shades, and leaned an arm on the truck window, filling the cab with peppermint fumes.

"Y'all got your pass? You should have it sitting on your dash."

I leaned over Todd, placing a hand over his to stop any upcoming tapping. "I'm the artist for the new visitor's center. There should be a work order in the office. Todd, what was the name?"

Todd slid his hands from mine, pulled a wrinkled paper out of his pocket, and consulted it. "Lonnie Harbaugh. Call him. He wrote up the work order."

"I hadn't heard about a painting job." The guard pulled a mini candy cane from his pocket and unwrapped it slowly.

"It's a big project," I said. "I've got a crew coming so we can get it done tonight. I'm kind of famous in Georgia for my ability to render a realistic drawing in a very short amount of time."

"You are?" said Priscilla. "Are you also famous for tooting your own horn?"

"What happened to that key?" I fierce-whispered.

Mister Gorilla Guard stuck the candy cane in the side of his mouth and took a long suck. "Well, now. I don't know nothing about that either. Y'all just sit here for a minute and let me check on this so-called painting project. You know you can't get to the rest of the exhibits from here."

"We aren't interested in seeing the Graceland exhibits," I said, dissuading any idea of us lying about an art project to get a free ride into Graceland at closing hours.

Which we weren't. We were lying about the art project for entirely different reasons.

The candy cane disappeared into the guard's minty cavern and reappeared on the other side of his mouth. "Why the hell not?"

"Why the hell not what, sir?" I asked politely.

"Why the hell aren't you interested in the Graceland exhibits? This is the King's home we're talking about."

"Because we're here to paint?" said Todd.

The guard blasted us with a peppermint-infused snort. "We'll just see about that." With a don't-you-move rap on the door, he stepped back and snatched his walkie-talkie from the belt holster.

While the Candy Cane Cop summoned Lonnie Harbaugh, I turned to Todd and Priscilla. "We better hope Byron's guy comes through. This guard takes his job a little too seriously."

"There's a lot of money riding on this game," said Todd. "It'll work."

"How much money are we talking about?" I mentally tallied my savings and checking accounts, which took no time with zero balances.

"These are pros, girl," said Priscilla. "They don't play for matchsticks and milk duds."

I let my head fall against Todd's brawny shoulder. "I will never understand why anyone would risk money on a game. If it wasn't for Byron, I'd never support the host of misdemeanors we are about to commit, including illegal gambling."

"The risk is what makes it fun." Todd nudged my head with his lips and circled my shoulders with his capable hands. "You should know that better than anyone."

"Well, isn't that sweet," said Priscilla. "You've buttered her up, Loverboy. Are you going to take a risk and see what she'll let you do? If we're caught, they're not going to let you share a cell. I can tell you that."

"You mean kiss Cherry?" said Todd.

"You should thank the Lord for making you pretty instead of smart. Did you want to kiss me instead?" said Priscilla. "Don't mind me. I'm gonna think about my job tonight and ignore whatever's going on in the front seat."

To save Todd's embarrassment, I allowed him a

minute of risky behavior before the guard waved us through the gate.

From my window, I watched another uniformed man take Candy Cane's spot at the entrance. The new guard tapped his nose as we drove past. Candy Cane gave our license plate a meaningful gander before strolling toward the construction office trailer.

BYRON and the Colonel met us at the service entrance of the new visitor's center. Boxes, lumber, and other building supplies filled the storage room.

Priscilla scanned the room with raised eyebrows and lips curled in doubt. "I sure hope this game is worth me canceling my Saturday night plans. It looks like the Home Depot exploded in here."

"Put a sock in it, Priscilla," said the Colonel. He pointed his cigar toward the open doorway in the back of the room. "Lonnie's got us set up in a conference room. We'll grab the rest of your supplies in a minute."

The heavy service doors shut behind us, cutting off the weak afternoon sunlight. With our arms full of Jupiter's painting supplies, Todd and I followed the Colonel down the dark hallway lined with taped drywall. Wires hung from openings in the ceiling and spackle dotted the cement floor.

"We're going to keep the front of the building locked off and feed everyone through the back door," explained the Colonel. "Anyone nosing around will think the newcomers are here to paint. Lonnie's got us set up all right."

"The guard seemed suspicious," I said. "I'm kind of nervous about this."

"That guy's an old timer," said Byron. "Lonnie says he goes off duty at five. Won't be a problem."

"Can't back out now," said the Colonel. "We've got plenty coming."

"What if the hustlers don't show?"

The Colonel shrugged. "Then Todd plays charity poker as planned. Byron will still get the house cut–after we deduct expenses. You better pray Todd can win more than his buy-in and house fee since he blew his wad losing at the tables in Arkansas."

"Wait a minute," I said. "What expenses? We wanted to attract the guys that scammed Byron."

"In order to attract our fish, we couldn't blab about Byron, now could we?" The Colonel stopped at the end of the dark hall and held open the door. "Those of us in the know will help Todd. If we can."

I eyed the Colonel, then maneuvered through the doorway. I didn't like the casual ruthlessness.

Seemed this Christmas sting had turned black op.

WHILE I THREW tarps on the ground and created an air of painterliness in the open area, the other men carried sections of a poker table and chairs into an empty room. Priscilla had disappeared, but I figured she didn't want to break another nail.

The area I was to pretend to paint was a central hub within the building. Rooms and hallways spoked off this nucleus. I visualized exhibits behind glass cases, perhaps a central desk with docents ready to assist the Elvis lovers in their pilgrimage.

Gazing at the walls, primed and ready for paint, I saw a medium prepared for my kind of genius. No way was I going to pretend to slap paint on this giant canvas, just in case a guard showed up. And no way could Chet rip up the sketches I was going to create on this giant canvas.

I grabbed the hardest lead pencil in my bag, a 2H, and a tape measure. "Hey Byron, would you mind bringing me a ladder?"

Byron popped out of the conference room, carrying a stepladder. "What'cha need, Cherry?"

"If you don't mind, can you follow me around the

room? We're going to make a series of crosses. I need you to help me hold the tape measure so I can mark off the lines."

"Crosses?" Byron gave me a look I recognized from folks who drank from half-empty glasses. "I thought you were supposed to pretend you're painting."

"This will be more helpful," I said. "You can save your 'told-you-so' for later, if I need it. I'll take full responsibility. I want to draw lines that are about three-by-three."

"Inches?"

"Why would I need a tape measure and ladder for inches? Feet, Byron. Three-by-three feet."

After a grumble, he circled the room with me. I drew light cross lines on the walls.

"Now what?" he said, squinting to see the crosses.

"For the next part, I'm going to grab an eraser and a softer lead. You're going to make sure nobody notices what I'm doing."

"Lord save us." Byron mopped his face with his hands, then smoothed his mustache. "I'm a nervous wreck and you're not helping. Can't you save your craziness for Vegas?"

"If I'm going to jail, I might as well make my mark here."

While I roughed out ovals, squares, and oblong rectangles around the cross lines, Byron donned coveralls, a painter's cap, and glasses. He found a corner, popped open the stepladder, and opened a can of paint to blend into our screen.

After my quick sketch of shapes, I peeked into the conference room. The Colonel and Priscilla huddled around a corner table. She shoved chips into a sorter while the Colonel fiddled with a laptop. At the long table set for twenty, Todd sat alone, drumming the felt top with his travel drumsticks.

"How's it going in here?" I sauntered toward Todd and leaned over him. Wrapping my arms around his shoulders, I placed my lips near his ear. "Are the Colonel and Priscilla doing anything that'd make me fret?"

He abandoned his drumsticks to reach behind my head and pull me closer, nuzzling my neck so I could hear his murmur. "Not that I can tell."

"Who's holding the money?"

"Priscilla's playing the house. They've got a software program to count down rounds and increase blinds. Makes the game more official-like."

As if her hearing was tuned to our sweet-nothings decibel, Priscilla looked up from her chip count and waved a pinky finger. "You ready for the big show, baby?"

I slid an exit kiss across Todd's lips, and he released me to continue drum practice. I strolled to the other side of the room, examining Priscilla's newest wardrobe change.

Her dark hair had returned to its towering '60s bouffant, but she wore a white fitted suit jacket with matching white slacks, blouse, and platform heels that spoke of the '70s. The sleek '70s style open collar blouse exposed more of her impressive cleavage.

"You changed again," I exclaimed. "You are definitely Priscilla tonight. From tip to toe. Monochrome really makes a statement."

"Of course," she beamed. "This is a genuine imitation of one of Ms. Presley's iconic looks. Except I mixed her early marriage hair with post-divorce apparel."

"Unusual for you to mix your Presley eras, isn't it?"

"I needed some help," she patted her bouffant. "You ruined my hair today after talking me into playing *Charlie's Angels*."

"Talking you into?" I huffed. "You're the one who insisted on coming along."

"I thought it'd be fun." She rolled her eyes. "I didn't realize there's a major difference between what you and I consider fun."

"Still, this outfit is pretty slick." I reached to stroke the wide lapel.

She flicked at my fingers. "Don't be getting your pencil smudges on my satin."

I studied the rainbow colored chips lying beneath her red-lacquered nails. "What's the highest amount you've got in there?"

She pointed to the shorter column of tangerine colored discs. "Ten thousand."

I inhaled my spit. Helpful as usual, the Colonel pounded on my back. Spinning around, I stared at Todd. "Ten thousand?"

"We've got a big buy-in. Going for long rounds and a slow blind increase. That'll help us the most. Don't want anybody getting too lucky." Todd shrugged, tapping the syncopated beat of *Jailhouse Rock*.

He spoke the language of poker more fluently than his mother-tongue of English. Yet any spark of intelligence effectively hid beneath his vacant, cerulean gaze. Todd did blank abstraction well.

Almost too well.

"When are they coming?" I asked.

"Anytime now." The Colonel flapped his hands at me. "If you're done necking with your boyfriend, make yourself useful and help the crowd find our room. Lonnie's people should be escorting them through the back."

Before I made it to the door, Todd's long arm snagged and reeled me into his side. "Don't worry, baby."

I snatched his drumsticks and slipped them into the deep pocket of my coveralls. "Maybe it's better if you don't drum tonight." I wondered if his nervous habit had blown the earlier games.

"Kiss for luck?"

Oddly enough, that kiss spoke more confidence than any words ever uttered from Todd's lips. Which wasn't saying much. But enough to give me hope.

ELEVEN
THE FADE

AS THE MOON rose over South Memphis, players from the tri-state region trickled into our makeshift parlor. Byron kept vigil in his back corner, covertly watching the players file in. With my HB pencil tucked behind my ear, I studied faces while ushering players into the conference room. I winked at Fred and Luther and whisked Jupiter into the room before he could study my wall art. Between greetings, I took a pencil to the wall and roughed in faces.

The next visitor made me itch to draw her face with crossed eyes, a mustache, and devil horns. But I'm bigger than marking up the Elvis Center's walls with nasty graffiti. I would save that illustration for Jupiter's sketchbook.

"It's going to be a long night." Lucinda patted her victory-rolled, cartoon red and black hair. "Hope you brought coffee for your guard duty."

"I hope you brought a sweater. It is December." I scowled at the polka dot print on her transparent blouse that barely hid her shoulder tats and lacy black bra.

"I imagine it'll heat up in that room pretty fast." She flashed a smirk from her pouty, scarlet mouth and swung into a chair next to Todd.

A handful of men walked into the room, giving me

no time for ugly thoughts about Lucinda. I glanced over my shoulder at Byron.

He brought a cigarette to his mouth and flipped open a zippo. The flame flared before his face.

I took another hard look at the three men. A hand landed on my shoulder. I gasped and slammed the conference room door shut. The hand tightened and spun me around, shoving me against the wall.

"What are you doing here?" growled Chet.

"Painting."

Little Jimmy stood beside Chet. Quick bursts of air labored from his open mouth. He squinted at me.

"This was the girl who drew pictures of the players last night," Chet said, recognizing Little Jimmy's lack of recall.

From the corner of my eye, I saw Byron slip out of the room.

"Right," said Little Jimmy. "The troublemaker."

The conference room door opened slightly. The Colonel poked his head out and spotted us. Sidling through the crack, he closed the door with his back. "Problem?"

Chet leaned against the wall, his shoulders rubbing against my pencil marks. "You tell me. You know this girl? She was in the Green Room last night."

"Sure. I know Cherry." The Colonel slipped a cigar from his pocket and pinched it between his fingers. "She's our visitor's gal."

"What's she doing out here?" said Chet.

"Hired her to pretend to paint the room. An added distraction to provide us some cover." Using his cigar as a pointer, the Colonel indicated the tarps and paint supplies.

"I don't trust her," said Chet. "She made a book of our faces."

"That feeling is mutual," I snarled. "The guys playing cards wanted their faces drawn. The book of faces was merely a sketchpad. An expensive one at that."

"Cherry's an artist." The Colonel shrugged off my affliction and shot me a look, warning me to keep my mouth shut. "I guess that's what she does when she's waiting for her man."

"Where's your sketchpad today?" said Chet.

"Don't have one." I met his scowl. "You shredded it, remember?"

"Are you going to play or what? Let's get this game started." The Colonel waved Chet toward the door and turned to Little Jimmy. "Are you playing tonight?"

"Little Jim's with me," said Chet. "He's here to protect my interests."

"I'd keep your eye on them, if I were you, Colonel," I said. "No telling what they're likely to rip up in that room."

"You stick to your paints, girl." The Colonel's cigar jabbed in my direction.

Once again, I held the overwhelming desire to snap the dang thing.

I waited until they had disappeared into the room before seeking Byron. He hid in an empty broom closet. "Did you recognize Chet or Little Jimmy? Chet's got one of those faces that blends into the crowd."

Before he could respond, we heard the distinct padding of footsteps down the concrete hall. Byron ran for his ladder. I grabbed a paintbrush.

A medium-built man with thinning hair loped into the room, packing a cigarette box against his hand. He dusted us with a disinterested gaze. A thin, weasel-faced man wearing cowboy boots and a trucker's cap scurried into the room behind him. I heard the snap and flick of Byron's lighter. Silently applauding my correct hunch, I smiled at the men and pointed toward the conference room door.

"That makes five," I said to Byron after the door

swung shut. "Do you know who that was? Elvis and the elf. The elf's wearing boots with lifts."

"Are you sure?"

"I sketched out their faces after following that van. Elvis obviously wears a wig and padding when he's singing. He didn't change the shape of his nose or the small scar on his chin."

I attended to my mural. Choosing a cross mark overlaid with an oval, I filled in full lips and a broad forehead jutting over small, dark eyes. I skimmed in a long nose and added a scar to the chin. In less than a minute, I had penciled in the basic features for the man who had just walked past me.

"Watch," I said to Byron. With the flat side of my soft, B4 pencil, I covered the top of the head with stylized hair, added sideburns, and drew in cartoonish glasses.

"Elvis lives."

HOURS LATER, my excitement had waned.

"Hell, this is boring," I said to Priscilla, pointing to Byron's curled and snoring body on the floor as proof.

"They've been sitting around that table for an eternity. Todd's got his back to me, so I can't see his chip pile over his scrumptious…" I paused. "Big shoulders. And every time I try to step into that room, I'm shushed and shoved out by the Colonel."

"These tournaments take time. I've seen them go on for days." Priscilla snagged a Red Bull from the community cooler and leaned against my angry elf portrait.

"Days?" If I had a beer in my hand like I wished, suds would have shot out of my nose. "We've got to catch the bus tomorrow morning."

"How many poker tournaments have you watched?"

"None."

"Not even on TV?" Priscilla gaped at me. "Not even the World Poker Tour?"

"Now that sounds real fun, watching poker on TV. Sounds about as exciting as watching bowling or fishing. Or paint drying, with which I do have experience. And for that, I walk away instead of watching it happen."

Priscilla's plucked and tinted brows rose toward her lofty bouffant. "What did you think you would do in Vegas?"

"I'm fixing to do quick sketches of the players at twenty bucks a pop. Just like I did in the Green Room."

"Are you planning on cutting out chunks from this wall at twenty bucks a pop?" She motioned to my drawings and slid to the floor.

I laughed and sat down beside her. "This was to alleviate my boredom. And to get back at the Colonel for making me stand guard. Don't worry. Before we leave, I'll paint over the pencil marks with the primer. Although, if someone saw a sketch they'd like, I'd be happy to work one up on paper or on a canvas and mail it to them."

"That'll cost more than twenty bucks," said Priscilla, digging another drink out of the cooler. She handed me a Coke. "Now, during the Vegas tournament, you can't be drawing folks. You can watch, though. But you'd have to be real quiet."

"Then I'd better wait at the pool and work on my tan."

"You're one of those girlfriends, huh?"

I gave Priscilla a hard, what're-you-talking-about look and popped the top on my Coke.

"Todd's your boy toy," she continued. "You're playing around until something better comes along and he doesn't know it."

"Who's talking about settling down? We're mostly friends, anyway."

"Friends with bennies never works, no matter what

the stories say. I guarantee that boy wants more than what you're willing to dish." She waved the energy drink can before my face. "I know these things, baby. You got another man in the wings, don't you?"

I shook my head and chugged my Coke.

"Oh, sugar, you are carrying some heavy baggage, aren't you? What happened to the other one?"

"He's a soldier. I don't expect to see him again."

"Honey, I can hear it in your voice. He done you so wrong." She sighed with the full dramatic license allotted to aging divas. "You're from Scarlett country, aren't you? You know that saying, 'After all, tomorrow is another day?' Let the past go and grab hold of those scrumptious shoulders of Todd's while you can."

"What about you? Why aren't you settled? It's not like you're some spring–"

She shot me a hard look.

"You know what I'm saying," I continued. "I can tell you're lonely, too."

"Lonely?" Her gaze wandered to the conference room door. She sighed. "I've got friends, just like you. My career isn't what I thought it was going to be, but I get to perform most nights and dress like my idol. It could be worse."

"You're working at the Heartache. I think it could be better."

"I've tried other places." She shrugged. "The Heartache suits me."

"The Colonel is at the Heartache."

"I guess we both have a penchant for the wrong men." She smiled. Her eyes had gone soft and dreamy. "There was a time when he was flush. He could really show a gal a good time, you know. I like a little showmanship. We've had some crazy fun. There's been some awesome ups with the downs."

"But…"

"But nothing." She fluttered her lashes at me.

"Lately, it's been more downs than ups. He is not the man I thought he was."

"Is he…" I tried to cast out the judgment from my voice. "Not good for you?"

"Well." She lifted a shoulder. "Even if it ain't all wine and roses, tell me what life is."

"My Grandma Jo and Grandpa Ed did pretty good. Their farm wasn't much. They had a simple life, but they were happy. Until Grandma Jo died," my voice faltered. "That happened when I was in high school."

"They raised you?"

"My momma … well, I'd say she wasn't content with the simple life."

"Not all of us are."

"She could have tried." I hated the sound of the whine in my voice. "It wasn't just her life. She dumped three kids on Grandma Jo and took off. There's a point where you need to take responsibility for the other people in your life."

"Kind of like how you need to take some responsibility for how you treat the blond angel in there who'd do anything for you?"

"That's not the same—"

The room exploded in blue uniforms and badges. I froze, my mouth still open. The Coke in my hand threatened to tip. I set it down and snapped my mouth shut.

Byron snorted, rolled over, and scrambled to his feet.

The Candy Cane Cop marched through the hall entrance behind the police and pointed at my resting spot on the floor. "There they are. Where's the blond guy who was with you? Where's the rest of your painting crew? I saw the vehicles parked nearby."

"Lord Almighty." Priscilla stood and smoothed her tuxedo. "I don't know what's going on. I'm just keeping these painters company while they take a break."

"You don't know what's going on?" Candy Cane growled. "So something *is* going on? And why are you so dressed up to keep some painters company?"

"I just stopped by to say hello. I'll get going." Priscilla edged toward the door. A cop standing at the back exit held up his hand to stop her.

Candy Cane turned his vengeful expression back on me. "I knew you were up to something. Lonnie must have faked that work order." He spun a slow circle around the room. "Look at this. Vandalism."

"I told you not to draw on the walls," hissed Byron.

"So she's the one who drew on the walls?" Candy Cane tapped the officer standing next to him. "Are you getting this down? This ain't even an Elvis mural, except for that one sketch. Who are these people in the drawings?"

"Ma'am," said Cop Number One. "You're going to need to come with us."

I couldn't move. I stared dumbfounded at the officer until he leaned over and hauled me to my feet. When the handcuffs zipped over my wrists, I found my wits.

"We're just a painting crew," I yelled. "Call Lonnie. He'll tell you. I'm an artist. I know I was just supposed to put color on the walls, but I couldn't help myself. They're so big and blank. I was gonna paint over them, I swear!"

"Where's the rest of your crew?" demanded Candy Cane. "There's got to be at least twenty people with you. Are you having a party or something? You better not be some of them Elvis haters, looking to embarrass the King."

I hoped Todd and the Colonel heard my bellowing and were currently directing the players out the conference room window. I also hoped the Colonel was on the phone, calling his buddy at the station.

"I'll go with you. This is all just a big misunderstanding," I hollered. "I'm sure we can get this cleared up at the station."

"Shut up. Why are you yelling?" Candy Cane tossed a ring of keys to Cop Number Two. "Start opening doors. Find the perps who belong to those vehicles."

"I knew we should have parked somewhere else," said Byron.

"Shush, Byron," I said.

The female officer unlocked the conference room door and pushed it open. "Here they are."

Cops Three and Four covered Number Two as she entered. The scuffle of a fight emerged behind the blue bodies blocking the doorway.

"Hold it right there," Number Two's voice rang out over the din. "You are all under arrest for trespassing."

I strained to see into the room, trying to catch sight of Todd or any who were left. The sounds of muffled voices, shuffling, and shoving carried into the outer room, but the police made an effective screen to the events happening inside.

"Y'all step this way until we're ready for you," said Cop Number One. He herded Byron, Priscilla, and me into an empty room. Closing the door, he locked us inside.

"Well, Miss Artist," said Priscilla. "I guess this didn't work out so good. Any more bright ideas?"

TWELVE
THE DEAD HAND

THIRTY MINUTES LATER, our heated tempers had warmed the December chill out of our small room better than a pot belly stove fired with coal.

"This is why I don't believe in charity events that don't have celebrity backers," said Priscilla. "If Wayne Newton ran this gig, we would not be thrown in the hoosegow."

"We're getting thrown in the hoosegow because gambling is illegal in the state of Tennessee," I said. "And if Byron had minded the law to begin with, none of this would have happened."

"You're the one who thought we should win my money back," said Byron.

"You both stopped being amusing about ten seconds after I met you," said Priscilla. "My limbs have been mangled all day because of your cleverness, Miss Amateur Artist. You probably gave me tendinitis. Squished in the back of a van and now cuffed like a common criminal? And Byron, you are just one sorry excuse."

Our makeshift jail door swung open and cut short the argument. Cop Number One's scowl doused the room with more ill humor. He jerked a thumb toward the center hall. We filed toward the door.

"What's going on?" I asked Number One, surveying

the Zip Tie-cuffed party standing in the hall. Apparently, not all of the players had escaped through the window of the conference room.

In the rotunda, Candy Cane Cop had unwrapped another stick of peppermint and toured the walls, examining my masterpieces. Jupiter and Fred must have gotten away, as well as Elvis and the Elf.

The remaining party hurled threats at the Colonel. The Colonel took those insults and threw them back at Todd. Chet, Little Jimmy, Luther, and Lucinda watched, wearing expressions better seen in a police lineup. Good practice, the way this night was headed.

Poor Todd stood with his head bowed and hands locked behind him, calmly suffering the arrows and daggers shot from the Colonel's mouth.

I scurried to defend my sweet gambler from the poisonous abuse directed his way.

"That girl should have paid better attention," screamed the Colonel. His hat sat askew and his bolo tie had loosened. The longhorn emblem dangled near the silver-tipped points. "She was supposed to be our lookout. Instead, she's drawing on the walls."

"This isn't Cherry's fault," said Todd. "Lonnie dropped the ball. He should've had us park somewhere different."

"Lonnie risked a lot just making up that work order. You're the idiots who came early and got the wrong guard at the gate."

"You said get here at four," said Todd.

"I said after four," fumed the Colonel.

I noticed Cop Number One's pen racing over his little notebook, getting the confessions word for word. If my hands weren't cuffed, I would have done another palm to the forehead.

My forehead had seen more abuse in two days than in my twenty-six years.

"Shut it, you two," I muttered. "Save it for the station."

"You," said the Colonel, turning on me. "I'm going to kill you."

"Don't mess with Cherry," said Todd, jumping in front of me.

"Sakes alive, that's romantic," exclaimed Priscilla. "But Miss Artist is right. Now, who was your little friend at the station, Colonel? I'd like to talk to him personally."

"Would you all just shut up?" said Lucinda. "The Colonel's little friend is not available for station visits, Priscilla."

"What do you mean?" She flashed a look at Little Jimmy. His eyes met hers with cold indifference.

Cop Number Three walked out of the conference room carrying the laptop, chips, and cards in ziplock bags.

"The money's gone." Todd swiveled his head to the Colonel. "You cheat."

"You should talk, wise guy," said Luther. "How did you win all those rounds? Funny how all weekend you lost hands until this tournament. Were you switching cards, you sandbagger?"

"I'm no cheat," said Todd. "Didn't you wonder how I won big enough online to get a trip to Vegas? I'm Sticks. You're the ones doing collusion and chip dumping. You and Elvis and the short guy."

Cop Number One scribbled furiously in his notebook. Cop Number Two snapped on gloves, placed her hands on her hips, and studied the remaining players.

"Sticks?" Lucinda's crimson pout dropped open as she stared at Todd. "You're Sticks?"

"Wait a minute," I said. "What is Sticks?"

"My online name," said Todd. "'Cause I'm a drummer, too."

"So why is everybody's jaw on the floor?"

"You don't know?" Lucinda sneered. "He's a legend in the online poker world." She turned back to Todd, swapping her look from contemptuous to cheeky. "I'm Rockabilly Girl, by the way."

"I know." He smiled. "I could tell by the way you only raise when you're holding aces."

My eyes narrowed. "You knew Lucinda before we came to Memphis?"

"Now baby," he said, "I only played against her on-line. That's all."

"Who's Elvis and the little guy?" asked Cop Number One, rereading his notes.

I pointed to their likeness on the wall with my cuffed hands. "I think you'll need to ask Little Jimmy and Luther where to find them. Or Priscilla, since she does bookings for them. You can check the maps at Venture Realty for the cities they've already hit. You'll find the towns that had a poker scam will match the Elvis shows. Priscilla doesn't play poker well enough to work that end of the scam."

Priscilla's head snapped toward me, knocking her bouffant askew. "You bitch."

"Sorry, but you dropped too many hints to the Colonel about making easy money." I gave her a pitying look. "The cut must be a lot better than what you can make at the Heartache. Is scamming people out of their savings really worth it just to continue your act?"

"I'm an artist, honey." She smoothed her tuxedo jacket. "I'll do this to the day I die."

"Might be coming soon," growled Little Jimmy. "You helped that drawing girl."

"I am also an *artist*," I said, making sure to empha-size the title for Little Jimmy's benefit. "And I get it. But I'm not about to beg, borrow, or steal to keep painting. I'm comfortable with an extremely modest income. For the most part."

"You say that, but you're not going to stay young forever. When you get to be my age, you'll think differ-ently." She glanced at Todd. "Unless you're looking for a different kind of bankroll. A permanent patron?"

"I never said that," I protested.

"What's wrong with a little permanency, Priscilla?" asked the Colonel. "We could have that."

"Too little, too late," Priscilla sniped. "Your sugar daddy days are behind you. If you give up the Heartache and make some real bank, give me a call."

"Give up the Heartache?" pleaded the Colonel. "What about our love of Elvis?"

"I could have taken my show on the road, but you insisted on investing in that crappy motel." She touched her hair. "I still look the part of my namesake. Maybe instead of sticking around here, waiting on you, I'll try my luck elsewhere."

My eyes narrowed. "Check her wig. It's held on with bobby pins, not glue."

"No one touches my hair," Priscilla shrieked.

Three cops bore down on her. Cop Number Two pulled out the bobby pins and lifted the bouffant. Reaching into the center of the beehive, she pulled out a giant wad of hair. The hair parted, revealing it had been expertly glued onto a fabric drawstring bag.

"Well, here's some of the money," said Cop Number Two, holding up folded hundreds. She deposited the money and bag into separate ziplock bags.

"Come on, let's see what else you're hiding." She shoved Priscilla toward the conference room. "I can search you nicely here. Or you can resist and we can do it at the station, which will not be so nice."

"Are you the realtor?" I said to Luther. "Somebody has to represent Venture when you get the keys to the empty offices. You've got a day job a few doors down from Venture Realty. Little Jimmy's working in the Green Room and drafting guys to play poker. They probably don't even know it's a scam, do they? Just an opportunity to have a little fun at some chump's expense."

Luther stared stonily at me.

I glanced at Byron. "Help us out. Use my sketches and point out who played poker with you at FBN."

Cop Number One uncuffed Byron. They circled the room. Byron tapped on the face of Elvis, then pointed at the Elf. "This was Mr. Smith."

At Chet's picture, he hesitated.

"What the hell," said Chet. "I'm not involved with these people. You're trying to set me up."

"Why'd you have Little Jimmy shred my good sketchbook?" I said.

He eyed Cop Number One's notebook and pressed his lips shut.

"Don't want to see any evidence connected to your underground business?" I looked at Byron. "Was it Chet?"

"Wasn't Chet," said Byron. He tapped on Fred's picture.

"Dang," I said. "I liked Fred. He had those cute dimples."

"Baby." Todd flashed me a look to remind me of his own dimples.

"How about Lucinda?"

"You wish," she said.

Priscilla and Cop Number Two returned from the conference room with a '60s-era corset. Priscilla winced as the policewoman pulled stacks of cash from customized pockets sewn into the front and back of the shapewear. Tossing the money in another ziplock, she placed the bag on the cooler with the other evidence she had collected.

"I can't believe the amount y'all are willing to risk on a game," I exclaimed. The money Priscilla held in her hair and girdle would have paid off my student loans and gotten me a decent used vehicle. "Now Byron's family is really sunk. A daddy spending Christmas in jail and not a penny to his name because of poker. I hope you learned something from this, Byron. You, too, Todd."

"It's not worth the risk without a big reward, baby." Todd shrugged. "If you don't understand, I can't explain."

"Come on." Cop Number One ushered Priscilla, Luther, and Little Jimmy toward the exit. "There's an escort waiting for you outside."

Priscilla buttoned her tuxedo jacket–one that no longer fit her tightly. Without the shapewear and bouffant, she looked younger. Only the graying roots of her tight bun betrayed her age. "What about them?"

"I'd focus on worrying about yourself just now," said Cop Number Three and gave her a soft push toward the door.

"We'll meet again, Miss Artist," called Priscilla over her shoulder. She stumbled out the door behind Little Jimmy and Luther.

"I hope so, Priscilla." Despite her criminal inclinations, I liked her. I hoped she'd learn to live on a smaller budget. And stop jonesing for the thrill of things like larceny. If she did, maybe she and the Colonel could settle down.

"What's going to happen to us? I wasn't involved in any scam," demanded Chet. "I had no idea we were trespassing."

Candy Cane Man sauntered from his corner observation spot to our group.

"Let him go," he said to Cop Number Three. "I won't press any charges on him or the woman. I want the instigators. The Colonel, the artist, the blond guy, and the other painter."

As Lucinda hurried past Todd, she made the international phone sign and winked. "Call me when you get out."

I would have said something, but I had more important considerations than jealousy. Like the fact that Todd, Byron, the Colonel, and I were cuffed and under police custody.

In the conference room, blue lights flashed through

the open window and played a disco pattern over my drawings in the hub. A December breeze drafted in, ruffling the paint tarps.

I shivered.

"Well, what can I say?" said the Colonel, his eyes fixed on the blue lights outside. "You win some, you lose some."

ABSORBED IN OUR OWN THOUGHTS, our small, cuffed group watched the blue lights disappear.

"You win some, you lose some." Todd's grin met his ears. "But I sure like winning better than losing."

Byron laughed. "I think you had to work harder at losing than you did at winning."

"And to think I made fun of you in high school for acting in all those school plays." Todd nudged him. "You can cry on cue better than a soap opera star."

"I will never understand poker," I said, shaking out my hands as Cop Number Two—also known as Marylou Draeger, Lonnie's receptionist—pulled the handcuffs off. "Man, those cuffs are uncomfortable. I hope I never have to wear them again."

"Really?" said Todd. "I thought I'd keep a pair and bring them to Vegas. We could have some fun…"

"Think again, smart guy," I said, but gave him a celebratory kiss that would have the extra effect of making him forget Lucinda.

I'm a believer in killing birds with as few stones as possible.

"Byron, collect Jupiter's stuff." Barry tossed his hat and tie to the floor, ridding himself of the Colonel, his Heartache Motel uniform. "He's coming back in thirty minutes to pick it up. We better get before the next shift comes on. Cherry, you need to get rid of those pencil marks. Lonnie, hurry up and count that money. We need to pay Byron and Todd back before we divvy up the rest."

"Sure thing," said Lonnie. The candy cane rotated around his lips. He pulled a handful of cellophane-wrapped treats from his pocket and handed one to me. "Want one?"

"Yes. Hell's bells, I'm starving." I looked at Barry. "I really had no idea how boring most of this night would be. We should have gotten this deal catered."

"You are too much," replied Barry. "I was sweating bullets as it was. I love a good thrill as much as the next guy, otherwise I wouldn't own the Heartache. Or play poker. But this sting near gave me a stroke."

"You had a great idea meeting up at the Heartache, Barry. You were right about Priscilla and her crew falling for a big game." I hugged him, then popped the candy cane into my mouth. "I'm sorry about Priscilla. Hope you can make it work out."

"Guess I'll have to book all new acts. She was a real showstopper." He sighed. "She liked that I played backroom poker and that sort of thing. But I couldn't get serious because I knew she never really wanted it. She's what they called a good time gal."

"You never know. She might change. A little scared straight might do it." I gave him another hug. "Anyway, we appreciate you doing all this for Byron. You're a good man."

"Byron, Lonnie, and I have been in the same fantasy football league since Byron moved here," said Barry. "Tina won't let Byron play the tables with me at the Green Room, but we've gotten to know each other pretty well during our league meetings and watching the games on Sunday."

"Yeah, thanks, Barry," said Byron. "I owe you and Lonnie big. Y'all get my first picks in the draft this year. Thank you, too, Todd and Cherry."

"Anything for my cousin," said Todd.

"We were going to Vegas, anyway," I said. "It's not like you have to beg Todd to play poker."

"I didn't know the real cops were coming," said Barry. "I thought I would lose my lunch. No one said anything about real cops in the original plan. Lonnie and I should have known about this days ago."

"I made a call home." I squeezed Todd's hand. "I know you thought real cops would scare everyone away, but the FBN scammers needed a greater punishment than just losing to you in a poker game. Uncle Will ran the pictures and sketches I faxed and collaborated with a detective in the Memphis PD. They found our charity poker tournament amusing, so we're not in trouble."

"Charity poker. Pretty much true," said Lonnie, smiling. He handed Byron a candy cane. "Guess you'll get out of the dog house yet."

"Still got to find a new job," said Byron. "But yeah, my kids will have full stockings this year, thanks to y'all. Mostly, it feels good to get even with those bastards."

"I bet you'll find that wedding ring in the Venture Realty's office safe," I said. "Or in the pawn shop next door."

"You're so smart, baby." Todd hooked an arm around my neck and kissed my head. "We've still got the *Blue Hawaii* suite for the rest of the night. Let's say we go back and I teach you my best poker moves."

I thought about Priscilla's words of wisdom on my ineptitude as a girlfriend. Even though she had no qualms about ripping off innocents at Christmas, she might have had a point when it came to relationships. I needed to let go of my tall, dark, and dimpled past and focus on a possible future of tall, blond, and dimpled.

Todd might not be ambitious or brilliant, but he did have interesting creative pursuits like music and making bucket loads of money off folks stupid enough to bet against him. He liked living in Halo and wanted to support my art career.

And, as it turned out, he was an excellent smoocher.

Not that I was trying to hook a husband. I wasn't ready to be that settled. Besides, could I trust myself to not pull a stunt like my mother?

"Guess we could practice a little *Viva Las Vegas* before the real deal," I said, stretching on tiptoes to meet his lips. "*Merry Christmas Baby.*"

He broke off the kiss to pin me with a blue-eyed gaze. "Thank you. Thank you very much."

The End. Until you read Portrait of a Dead Guy, the first Cherry Tucker Mystery novel.

READY FOR MORE CHERRY TUCKER? Continue reading for a one chapter preview!

ON WRITING QUICK SKETCH

Although *Quick Sketch* is a prequel to *Portrait of a Dead Guy*, the first in my Cherry Tucker Mysteries, I wrote it between my third and fourth mysteries. At the time, I was chatting (horsing around) with two of my Henery Press writer friends, Terri L. Austin and LynDee Walker, about how much fun it would be to put our three amateur sleuths together. Because our characters lived in Kansas City, Missouri; Richmond, Virginia; and Halo, Georgia, it felt quite a feat to get them together.

That's how Memphis evolved. It would seem all the characters would have a reason to visit Graceland, and we took that idea to our editor. To date, it's the only time Cherry Tucker (fictionally) leaves Georgia in one of my novels.

We didn't realize that although our characters would all stay at the same hotel, they would never meet. However, we had a great time coming up with all the characters who would work at the notorious *Heartache Motel*, the eponymous name for the anthology where our stories appeared.

For my part, I wanted to write a sting rather than a straight-up mystery. I've always loved con artist stories. A seedy motel like the Heartache seemed the perfect place for a long con. *The Sting* and *Paper Moon* were two of my favorite movies as a kid.

The con that Byron fell for was actually based on a real scam. When I first wrote this story, my editor couldn't believe it. Which goes to show you, truth is stranger than fiction!

Years later, I would take my love of con artist stories and create a new character, Finley Goodhart. I'm including an excerpt of her first book, *The Cupid Caper*, at the end of this one, as well as the preview for Cherry Tucker's first mystery, *Portrait of a Dead Guy*.

If you'd like to have Finley Goodhart's prequel–the short story, *The Pig'n a Poke*–it's my gift to my VIP Readers' penpal group. You can sign up to get *The Pig'n a Poke* and unsubscribe if you don't want to stay. :) Just go to my website and tap the big pink button at the top or type in this link in your browser:

LarissaReinhart.com

You'll be the first to learn of my new releases, my upcoming projects, and exclusive giveaways, including bonus content, monthly drawings, free downloads, and signed book giveaways at each new release.

I hope you enjoyed *A Christmas Quick Sketch*!

Happy Reading!

Larissa

HAVE YOU READ A PORTRAIT OF A DEAD GUY?
SNEAK PEEK AT CHAPTER 1

IN A SMALL TOWN, there is a thin gray line between personal freedom and public ruin. Everyone knows your business without even trying. Folks act polite all the while remembering every stupid thing you've done in your life. Not to mention getting tied to all the dumbass stuff your relations — even those dead or gone — have done. We forgive but don't forget.

I thought the name Cherry Tucker carried some respectability as an artist in my hometown of Halo. I actually chose to live in rural Georgia. I could have sought a loft apartment in Atlanta where people appreciate your talent to paint nudes in classical poses, but I like my town and most of the three thousand or so people that live in it. Even though most of Halo wouldn't know a Picasso from a plate of spaghetti.

Still, it's a nice town full of nice people and a lot cheaper to live in than Atlanta. Halo citizens might buy their living room art from the guy who hawks motel overstock in front of the Winn-Dixie, but they also love personalized mementos. Portraits of their kids and their dogs, architectural photos of their homes and gardens, poster-size photos of their trips to Daytona and Disney World. God bless them.

That's my specialty, portraits.

But at this point, I'd paint the side of a barn to make

some money. I'm this close from working the night shift at the Waffle Hut. And if I had to wear one of those starchy, brown uniforms day after day, a little part of my soul would die.

Actually, a big part of my soul would die because I'd shoot myself first.

When I heard the high falutin Bransons wanted to commission a portrait of Dustin, their recently deceased thug son, I hightailed it to Cooper's Funeral Home. I assumed they hadn't called me for the commission yet because the shock of Dustin's murder rendered them senseless. After all, what kind of crazy called for a portrait of their murdered boy? But then, important members of a small community could get away with little eccentricities.

I was in no position to judge. I needed the money.

After Dustin's death made the paper three days ago, there'd been a lot of teeth-sucking and head-shaking in town, but no surprise at Dustin's untimely demise from questionable circumstances. It was going to be that or the State Pen. Dustin had been a criminal in the making for twenty-seven years.

Not that I'd share my observations with the Bransons. Good customer service is important for starving artists if we want to get over that whole starving thing.

As if to remind me, my stomach responded with a sound similar to a lawnmower hitting a chunk of wood. Luckily, the metallic knocking in the long-suffering Datsun engine of my pickup drowned out the hunger rumblings of my tummy.

My poor truck shuddered into Cooper's Funeral Home parking lot in a flurry of flaking yellow paint, jerking and gasping in what sounded like a death rattle. However, I needed her to hang on. After a couple of big commissions, hopefully, the Datsun could go to the big junkyard in the sky.

My little yellow workhorse deserved to rest in peace.

I entered the Victorian monstrosity that is Cooper's,

leaving my portfolio case in the truck. I made a quick scan of the lobby and headed toward the first viewing room on the right. A sizable group of Bransons huddled in a corner. Sporadic groupings of flower arrangements sat around the narrow room, though the viewing didn't start until tomorrow.

A plump woman in her early fifties, hair colored and highlighted sunshine blonde, spun around in kitten heel mules and pulled me into her considerably soft chest. Wanda Branson, stepmother to the deceased, was a hugger. As a kid, I spent many a Sunday School smothered in Miss Wanda's loving arms.

"Cherry!" She rocked me into a deeper hug. "What are you doing here? It's so nice to see you. You can't believe how hard these past few days have been for us." Wanda began sobbing. I continued to rock with her, patting her back while I eased my face out of the ample bosom.

"I'm glad I can help." The turquoise and salmon print silk top muffled my voice. I extricated myself and patted her arm. "It was a shock to hear about Dustin's passing. I remember him from high school."

I remembered him, all right. I remembered hiding from the already notorious Dustin as a freshman and all through high school. Of course, that's water under the bridge now, since he's dead and all.

"It's so sweet of you to come."

"Now Miss Wanda, why don't we find you a place to sit? You tell me exactly what you want, and I'll take notes. How about the lobby? There are some chairs out there. Or outside? It's a beautiful morning and the fresh air might do you good."

"I'm not sure what you mean," said Wanda. "Tell you what I want?"

"For the portrait. Dustin's portrait."

"Is there a problem?" An older gentleman in a golf shirt and khaki slacks eyed me while running a hand through his thinning salt-and-pepper hair. John Branson, locally known as JB, strode to his wife's side. "You're Cherry Tucker, Ed Ballard's granddaughter, right?"

I nodded, whipping out a business card.

He glanced at it and looked me over. I had the feeling JB wasn't expecting this little bitty girl with fly-away blonde hair and cornflower blue eyes. My local customers find my appearance disappointing. I think they expected me to return from art school looking as if I walked out of 1920s bohemian Paris wearing black, slouchy clothes and a ridiculous beret.

I like color and a little bling myself. However, I toned it down for this occasion and chose jeans and a soft orange tee with sequins circling the collar.

"Yes sir," I said, shaking his hand. "I got here as soon as I could. I'm sorry about Dustin."

"Why exactly did you come?" JB spoke calmly but with distaste, as if he held something bitter on his tongue. Probably the idea of me painting his dead son.

"To do the portrait, of course. I figured the sooner I got here, the sooner I could get started. I am pretty fast. You probably heard about my time in high school as a Six Flags quick sketch artist. But time is money, the way I look at it. You'll want your painting sooner than later."

"Cherry, honey, I think there's been some kind of misunderstanding." Wanda looped her arm around JB's elbow.

"JB's niece Shawna is doing the painting."

"Shawna Branson?" I would have keeled over if I hadn't been at Cooper's and worried someone might pop me in a coffin.

Shawna was a smooth-talking Amazonian poacher who wrestled me for the last piece of cake at a church picnic some fifteen years ago. Although she was three heads taller, my scrappy tenacity and love of sugar helped me win. Shawna marked that day as a chal-lenge to defeat me at every turn. In high school, she stole my leather jacket, slept with my boyfriend, and brown-nosed my teachers. She didn't even go to my school.

And now she was after my commission.

"She's driving over from Line Creek today," Wanda said. "You know, she got her degree from Georgia Southern and started a business. She's very busy, but she thinks she can make the time for us."

"I've seen her work," I said. "Lots of hearts, polka dots, and those curlicue letters you monogram on everything."

"Oh yes," said Wanda, showing her fondness for curlicue letters. "She's very talented."

"But ma'am. Can she paint a portrait? I have credentials. I'm a graduate of SCAD, Savannah College of Art and Design. I'm formally trained in mixing color, using light, creating perspective, not to mention the hours spent with live models. I can do curlicue. But don't you want more than curlicue?"

Wanda relaxed her grip on JB's arm. Her eyes wandered to the floral arrangements, considering.

"I have the skill and the eye for portraiture," I continued. "And this is Dustin's final portrait. Don't you want an expert to handle his precious memory?"

"She does have a point, JB," Wanda conceded.

JB grunted. "The whole idea is damn foolish."

Wanda blushed and fidgeted with JB's sleeve.

"The Victorians used to wear a cameo pin with a lock of their deceased's hair in it," I said, glad to reference my last-minute research as I defended her. "It was considered a memorial. When photography became popular, some propped up the dead for one last picture."

"Exactly. Besides, this is a painting, not a photograph," said Wanda. "It's been hard. I wanted to be closer to Dustin. JB did, too, in his way. And then Dustin was taken before his time."

I detected an eye roll from JB. Money wasn't the issue. Propriety needled him. Wanda loved to spend JB's money, and he encouraged her. JB's problem wasn't that Wanda was flashy; she just shopped above her raising. Which can have unfortunate results. Like hiring someone to paint her dead stepson.

"A somber representation of your son could be comforting," I said. Not that I believed it for a minute.

"Do you need the work, honey?" Wanda asked. "I want to do a memory box. You know, pick up one of those frames at the Crafty Corner for his mementos. You could do that."

"I'll do the memory box," I said. "I've done some flag cases, so a memory box will be no problem. But I really think you should reconsider Shawna for the painting."

"Now lookee here," said JB. "Shawna's my niece."

"Let me get my portfolio," I said. Pictures speak louder than words, and it looked like JB needed more convincing.

I dashed out of the viewing room and took a deep breath to regain some composure. I couldn't let Shawna Branson steal my commission. The Bransons needed this portrait done right. Who knows what kind of paint slaughter Shawna would commit? As far as I was concerned, she could keep her curlicue business as long as she left the real art to me.

My bright yellow pickup glowed like a radiant beacon in the sea of black, silver, and white cars. I opened the driver door with a yank, cursing a patch of rust growing around the lock.

Standing on my toes, I reached for the portfolio bag on the passenger side. The stretch tipped me off my toes and splayed me flat across the bench.

"I recognize this truck." A lazy voice floated behind me. "And the view. Doesn't look like much's changed either way in ten years."

I gasped and crawled out.

Luke Harper, Dustin's step-brother.

I had forgotten that twig on the Branson family tree.

More like snapped it from my memory. His lanky stance blocked the open truck door. One hand splayed against my side window. His other wrist lay propped over the top of my door.

Within the cage of Luke's arms, we examined each other. Fondness didn't dwell in my eyes. I'm never sure what dwelled in his.

Luke drove me crazy in ways I didn't appreciate. He knew how to push buttons that switched me from tough to soft, smart to dumb. Beautiful men were my kryptonite. Local gossip said my mother had the same problem. My poor sister, Casey, was just as inflicted. We would have been better off inheriting a squinty eye or a duckwalk.

"Hello, Luke Harper." I tried not to sound snide.

Drawing up to my fullest five foot and a half inches, I cocked a hip in casual belligerence.

"How's it going, Cherry?" A glint of light sparked his smoky eyes, and I expected it corresponded with a certain memory of a nineteen-year-old me wearing a pair of red cowboy boots and not much else. "You hanging out at funeral homes now? Never took you for a necrophiliac."

This time I gave Luke my best what-the-hell redneck glare. Crossing my arms, I took a tiny step forward in the trapped space. He stared at me with a faint smile tugging the corners of his mouth.

If I could paint those gorgeous curls and long sideburns — which will never happen, by the way — I would use a rich, raw umber with burnt sienna highlights. For his eyes, I'd mix Prussian blue and a teensy Napthal red. However, he would call his hair "plain old dark brown" and eyes "gray."

But, what does he know? Not much about art, I can tell you that.

"I thought you were in Afghanistan or Alabama," I said. "What are you doing back?"

"Discharged. You still mad at me? It's been a while."

"Mad? I barely remember the last time I saw you." I wasn't really lying. My last memory wasn't of seeing him, but seeing the piece of trash in his truck. And by piece of trash, I mean the kind with boobs.

"You were pretty mad at the time. And I know you and your grudges."

"I've got more to do than think about something that happened when I was barely out of high school."

"Are you going to hold my youthful indiscretions against me now?" He smiled. "I'm only in town for a short time. You know I can only take Halo in small doses."

"If you're not sticking around, I can't see how my opinion of you matters. Not like you asked me about your sudden decision to join the Army and clear out of dodge."

"That's what you're mad about?"

Dear God, men are clueless. Why He didn't sharpen them up a bit has to be one of life's greatest mysteries.

"There are a number of things you did. But I'm not about to print you out a list."

"We had some good times, too."

"Which you sabotaged with your idiocy."

"You're one to talk," he mumbled.

I took another step forward, but Luke didn't move. His eyes roamed from my face to my boots. My irritation grew.

"Do you mind? I need to get back to Cooper's. I'm working." I shoved him out of the way, dragging my unwieldy portfolio bag behind me.

"Just trying to put my finger on what about you changed."

I clamped my mouth shut as an unwelcome blush crept up the back of my neck.

"I know," he continued. "Your boots are plain old brown. Where're those red cowboy boots?"

I stomped toward the funeral home. "At home with

my Backstreet Boys albums. I don't have time to play catch up with you. I've got stuff to do."

"How about playing catch-up later, then?" I glanced back to see a glimmer of a smile. "Don't you think it'd be fun to stroll down memory lane? Does everybody still hang out at Red's?"

The sunlight played with the auburn highlights in his dark curls and the tips of his long, black eyelashes.

Lord, why does he have to be so good-looking? It was incredibly unfair how easily beauty weakened me. Gave suffering for art a whole new meaning.

"It was seven years ago," I said before I could stop myself. "What?"

"Not ten years," I corrected. "But a lot has happened in seven."

"I bet."

I FOUND Wanda shredding a tissue in the viewing room, watching JB bark orders at the assorted non-nuclear Bransons who then cowed and scurried as if he were the king of Forks County. He owned many businesses that supported most of the Branson clan, including the big Ford dealership, but he had inherited the Branson patrilineal power seat.

Ironically, the two Bransons who never bowed to JB were his son, Dustin, and stepson, Luke. And that was where the similarities between Dustin and Luke stopped.

Luke and Dustin were never close. Luke loved his mother and put up with Dustin when she remarried. However, Luke got out of Halo as soon as possible. Couldn't blame him, with a cold stepfather and a mother pouring her attention into rehabilitating an emerging sociopath. But poor Wanda had her hands full.

Made me wonder, though. With Dustin out of the picture, was there now more room for Luke? Interesting that Luke left the Army right when his step-brother got offed.

Hating that ugly thought, I hurried over to Wanda. "I just ran into Luke," I said, giving her shoulder a quick hug.

"I'm glad to see he's here to help you through this."

"Yes, it is a blessing. Served his time, you know, and of course, he won't tell me his plans yet. But that's Luke. Doesn't like to worry me."

"Keeps his cards pretty close to his chest, does he?"

"Look at him," Wanda waved at her son. "I've never been able to tell what he's thinking. Just like his father, God bless him. Maybe it was losing his daddy so young. He just keeps everything clammed up inside."

Spotting his mother's wave, Luke wandered into the viewing room. He had always been a wiry guy, displaying his strength in high school on the wrestling team and fighting behind the Highway 19 Quik Stop with the other boys carrying boulder-size chips on their shoulders. He still seemed dangerous, yet more settled and confident.

There was no softness about him. Luke was all hard edges.

"Oh, I don't know," I murmured. "I lost my daddy young, too, but I've always been an open book."

"Well, boys and girls are different," said Wanda.

"Don't I know it." I swung one palm to my hip but waved my other in casual deference to Luke's arrival. "Let's go sit, and you can take a look at my portfolio. While you're looking at my samples, I'll sketch some ideas I have for Dustin."

"What's this?" Luke asked. "Ideas for Dustin?"

"I'm having Dustin's portrait done," Wanda explained.

"I'll hang it next to the painting of him as a child. That one's thirty-by-forty. I'd like them to be the same size."

Holy cow, that's a big picture of a dead guy, I

thought but nodded my head as if it was the most reasonable idea in the world.

"That's downright morbid." Although he directed the statement to his mother, the accusation lay at my feet. "I swear you haven't changed Cherry, with all the nutty art stuff."

I felt like telling Luke, "This is your mother's crazy notion, not mine." Instead, I responded in my most proper aren't-you-an-idiot drawl, "Your momma is just dealing with this horrible tragedy the best she can, God bless her. It's a memorial."

"A memorial for Dustin? You don't know what Dustin was mixed up in, Mom. Death doesn't turn a sinner into a saint. God knows you tried your best. More than his father did."

"Come on, Miss Wanda," I tugged on her arm. Between Luke and Shawna, I was going to lose this commission. "I'll get you a cup of tea, and you can look at my paintings. It'll get your mind off things for a minute, anyway. I've got a real cute one of Snug, Terrell Jacob's Coonhound."

Wanda beckoned JB, and they conferred for a moment. With a shrug, he followed her out of the viewing room.

Luke shoved his hands in his pockets. "You spent all that money on art school to paint pictures of dogs?"

"I spent all that money on art school to become a professional artist," I said. "It's early days yet. For now, I take what I can get."

"Including painting the departed?"

"You ever heard of a still life?" I shot back and stalked out of the viewing room, swinging my portfolio bag behind me.

I followed Wanda and JB into a little room crowded with a table and chairs. Unzipping the large bag, I pulled out a binder of photographs of my college works and a sheaf of plastic-encased photos of my newer stuff. Snug the dog, a horse named Conquering Hero, and a half-dozen kid portraits. I much preferred animals to children as subjects, something you don't learn in school.

Getting a four-year-old to sit still is damn near impossible. However, you take a well-trained dog in the right pose, and you've got the perfect model. Snug the Coonhound sat better than most people. We had an easy working relationship, what with Snug's deferential silence. No need for forced conversation with that subject.

Of course with this job, I couldn't expect any conversation either. I could make do with photographs.

But first I needed to get the job.

"I don't know why you're wasting my time looking at pictures," said JB. He tossed the portraits of Snug and Hero on the table.

"This one is just beautiful, Cherry," said Wanda, holding up a Sargent-inspired painting. The model wore a sheet draped like a toga, but the effect was tasteful with wonderful folds to show depth and shadow.

"I'm glad you pointed out that one. Don't you love the light on her face? You might not be able to tell, but that's not an oil painting. I had a tight schedule, so I used acrylics. They dry quickly, and I didn't have to varnish the painting immediately. Someone mentioned you displaying the portrait at the funeral service? Oils wouldn't dry fast enough to get the painting done without messing up the color."

"I was fixing on making a photo display for the service when I realized we didn't have many of Dustin after he passed a certain age." Wanda's face colored and she cast her eyes away from JB. "I've just been in a tizzy, not knowing what to do with myself and not sleeping. That's when I got the idea for the memory box. Started gathering stuff Dustin left in his old room. Then I remembered the family portraits we had done at our wedding and thought maybe a new painting would be a nice tribute."

"Let her have what she needs," said JB. "A picture's not bringing him back, but if it makes Wanda feel better, she can have it."

"I totally agree, sir," I said. "That's why you should let me have the honor of painting this portrait. You can see what quality I can produce. You don't want a final memorial done by an amateur."

"What about Shawna?" he said, eyeing me. "Although Shawna did set a pretty hefty price for painting my son."

I squirmed, caught between a rock and a rattlesnake. JB would sell out his niece for a lower price. But probably wouldn't help me underbid her, either.

"A portrait lasts for generations." I began with my salesman pitch. "My paintings are heirloom quality and will be around long after…" Since the subject was dead, I stopped before my mouth ate my foot. "Anyway, a portrait is priceless."

"Priceless? You talking free?" JB leaned back in his chair.

"Of course, a professional artist would base the price on other features. Number of people. Intricacy of the clothing, jewelry, and props. Complexity of the background. And of course, the size." I could not get over the size.

"How complex is a coffin?" He steepled his hands under his chin. "And we don't need background details."

"JB, don't be cheap," said Wanda. "Like Cherry said, we're talking heirloom quality."

"Who in the hell wants to inherit a picture of Dustin in a coffin, Wanda?" JB said. "Even if little Dustins start crawling out of the woodwork, and God help us if that happens, I'm sure none of them will want this painting. We can cut some corners, here."

"Coffin portrait?" I said, swallowing hard. My mouth went dry, and I had trouble getting my tongue to form intelligible words. "I thought you'd want me to work from snapshots or something. Dustin standing in a field, looking off to heaven, that sort of thing."

"Oh no," said Wanda. "That would be phony. Dustin never would have stood in a field unless he was hunting, and I doubt he thought about heaven much."

She cast a quick look at her husband. "I want him as he is now. And realistic. None of that abstract stuff."

I gulped. "As he is now." The man was murdered. An abstract would be easier to stomach. Not like anyone would enjoy looking at David's *The Death of Marat* in their TV room. "All right. Uh, do you want me to create a pose, or do you want the whole, um, coffin?"

"Could you paint it like we were looking down at Dustin? Like angels gazing?" Wanda's moist blue eyes stared off into the distance, and I shivered.

I grabbed my notebook and made a quick sketch. "Something like this?" I showed her the rough illustration of my idea.

"Oh, it's just perfect," she said, grabbing the sketchbook to shove at JB. "Let's give Cherry a chance, honey. I want this view. Shawna said she has an allergy to formaldehyde so she couldn't paint Dustin this way."

"Tell you what." JB leaned forward, hands flat on the table. "I'll give you a shot. I want Wanda to be happy after what all she's endured with Dustin. He was my son and I owe her that."

"Yes, sir," I said, although my skin still prickled from the word formaldehyde.

"But," he said, "you got to have the painting done for the funeral. The whole shebang. Wanda can choose between you and Shawna, so you better make it good. She likes quality.

"After the funeral, I'm done. Wanda can hang up his picture and look at it all she wants, but I'm putting this whole blasted deal out of my mind. I'm paying off his creditors right and left, dealing with folks' complaints, and living through the embarrassment of the way he went. Do you know what they are saying about him?"

I knew, but I sure wasn't going to say. Folks thought a bad drug deal or payback from a robbery ring. Or someone just got tired of Dustin's mouth and went postal on him.

Hard to say with Dustin. There were so many crimes to choose from.

"I'll work up a contract," I said. "Thank you for this opportunity. I'll get cracking right away, and I'll also do the memory box."

"We'll have Cooper set out the body for you then." JB didn't smile, but I did see a flash of teeth. "Got to admire your tenacity, Cherry. I hate to say it, but stories I heard about your family made me question your reliability."

A shot of heat worked its way from my toes to my scalp. People always bring up my family's history over the years, but it never got any easier.

"My reputation is important to me. I am judged by my actions as well as those that surround me. You know how people like to talk."

"Yes, sir."

He looked at me evenly. "I'm glad we agree on this issue. As a businesswoman, you have your reputation to protect and a lot of history to overcome."

A million comebacks crossed my mind, but none were appropriate for a bereaved father sitting in a funeral home with a large check that could have my name on it.

I swallowed my pride and tried not to choke. "I'll bring that contract by tomorrow."

He had better keep his end of the bargain because, after that humiliation, I sure as hell wasn't working for free.

"LAUGH-OUT-LOUD FUNNY AND AS SOUTHERN AS SWEET TEA AND CHEESE GRITS"

Meet Cherry Tucker, big in mouth, small in stature, and able to sketch a portrait faster than kudzu climbs telephone poles! A 2012 Daphne du Maurier finalist, a 2012 The Emily finalist, a 2011 Dixie Kane Memorial winner, and a Woman's World Magazine book club pick for 2018!

"*Portrait of a Dead Guy* is an entertaining mystery full of quirky characters and solid plotting...Highly recommended for anyone who likes their mysteries strong and their mint juleps stronger!"

JENNIE BENTLEY, *NEW YORK TIMES* BESTSELLING AUTHOR OF *FLIPPED OUT*

In Halo, Georgia, folks know Cherry Tucker as big in mouth, small in stature, and able to sketch a portrait faster than buckshot rips from a ten gauge — but commissions are scarce. So when the well-heeled Branson family wants to memorialize their murdered son in a coffin portrait, Cherry scrambles to win their patronage from her small town rival.

As the clock ticks toward the deadline, Cherry faces more trouble than just a controversial subject. Between ex-boyfriends, her flaky family, an illegal gambling ring, and outwitting a killer on a spree, Cherry finds herself painted into a corner she'll be lucky to survive.

THE CUPID CAPER (CHAPTER ONE)
THE APPROACH

WEDNESDAYS OFTEN BROUGHT the college boys to Jello's Pool Hall. Particularly in the winter. I'd call it cabin fever, except we were in Georgia. Still, too cold to drink on their frat house front porch rocking chairs. Too early in the week to host a party. The non-heathens would be attending Wednesday night church. The good students would be in class or the library.

But the bad boys would bring money to places like Jello's. Which was why I was there.

And how Lex knew to find me.

I had just racked a fresh round. Satisfied with the smooth lift of the triangle. No balls escaped. Feeling good about the roll of twenties tucked into the front pocket of my jeans. That gratification disappeared upon sensing a male presence behind me. The scent of his aftershave cut through the pervading smell of beer, stale smoke, and old fryer oil. I sniffed once. Recognized the spicy scent of his cologne. Rested the cue stick on the table.

"Wanna make a wager? I'm having a lucky night." I bent over the table to place the cue ball. Angled the stick. Shot it backward. And turned to face him.

"Hello, love." Lex grabbed the stick. "Watch yourself. I'd like to remain a baritone, if you don't mind."

"Sorry." I didn't sound sorry. Didn't even get close.

"Careful where you stand next time. Another town, maybe?"

He pushed the stick away. Grinned. Sidled forward. "Don't want me too deep in your pocket?"

I rolled my eyes, then studied the man. His thick, sandy hair had been trimmed to maintain an artful dishevelment. Smiling blue eyes. Sensuous lips held a relaxed smile. His boy-next-door good looks never revealed anything but indolent charm and false promises. A real ace. Too careful and too practiced to show anything else.

"You look tired." I took a careful step to the side. Rested my hip against the table. "Tinge of blue beneath your eyes."

"Too many lonely nights."

"I bet. They have medicine for that, you know."

"Not the cure I seek. You're looking fit, though." His gaze traveled the room. "How'd you do tonight?"

"What do you want, Lex?" My hand reached for the cue ball. I rolled it beneath my palm.

His eyes snapped back to me and told me what I already knew. I narrowed mine. His mouth quirked.

"Relax," he said. "Gave you my word I'd leave you alone, didn't I?"

"Your word isn't worth much. And you just proved it, seeing as how you're here and all."

"When have I ever lied to you?"

I gripped the cue ball.

He raised his hand. "Right. But I am here out of the goodness of my heart. Thought I should see you about Penny Forbes."

"What about Penny?" I frowned. "Are you working together? Not interested."

"You haven't heard?" The mask fell. His face tightened and he appeared older, matured. "Fin, we should go somewhere private."

"Why?" I didn't like the mask, but I didn't like what he'd replaced it with either. He looked worried. Lex never worried. The carefree charisma wasn't just an act. I was the worrier. "You know I'm on the square now. If you and Penny have gotten yourself into a mess, y'all just get yourselves out of it."

"On the level, but still dodgy enough to plunder these wankers," he muttered. "Finley, I'm serious. I don't want to tell you here."

"You're never serious." I turned. Settled the white ball. Chalked the cue tip. Moved to the side and leaned over the table. Sighted the ball. Placed the stick between my thumb and fingers.

Lex leaned over me, close enough for his words to buzz in my ear. "She's dead, Fin. Penny's dead." A hand fell on my shoulder. "I'm sorry. I didn't want to tell you like this. Finley, come with me."

I pulled in a breath. Ignored his hand and the clamor ringing between my ears. Gritting my teeth, I lowered my head. Centered my gaze on the space between the second and fourth racked ball. Brought the stick back and let it glide. The break rang. Two solids slammed into the back and corner right pockets.

Lex's hand shot forward. Caught a stripe as it raced toward the front left. "Sloppy. That's a scratch."

"Hey." I turned, swinging the stick with me.

He caught the stick again, pushed it aside, and grabbed my arm. "Love, did you hear me? I'm sorry. I didn't want to be the bearer, but God knows I can't... I had to see you. News like this. I cocked it up." He shook his head. "Fin. Are you all right? What can I do, love?"

"Nothing." I shook my arm free and fixed my eyes to a point on the wall behind him. I hadn't seen Penny for months. She'd been busy. I'd been hiding. But dead? She was too young—mid-twenties, like me. Car accident? Cripes, I hoped she didn't get sick. The fatal illnesses I knew that struck Penny's age bracket weren't pretty.

I sucked in a deep breath. Let it out. Hated how shaky it sounded. "How'd she die?"

"Let's talk somewhere else." He paused. Sighed. "Right. Drug overdose. Heroin, is what I heard."

My eyes flew to his face. The blue eyes watched me. Soberly, with a hint of pity. I despised that look even more than the worry.

"No way on God's green earth. Penny's momma was a junkie. Crooked as she could get, Penny wouldn't touch a substance stronger than champagne. You heard wrong, Lex."

He shrugged. "I'm sorry, love."

"Stop calling me that." I felt my throat tighten and forced a swallow. "Don't call me that anymore."

"Can't help myself." His head tilted, the pitying expression deepening. "Let me at least buy you a drink. We should toast Penny. You've known her since, when? First time on the street?"

He reached for me, but I sidestepped. "I'm not drinking to that lie. She didn't overdose."

"Fin, it's hard to hear, but it's true. Heard it from Dot, then checked myself."

"Who found her?" I gripped my cue stick. My chest felt like it was going to cave in. "Police? Which one? County? City? The heroin could have been planted, Lex. You know she's on *his* list because of me. It's not beneath him to do something like that just to make her look bad. He's got the county coroner in his pocket. John Prince is a drunk and a gambler—"

"What would be the point in that? Penny was taken to the hospital, love. Wasn't a bust or anything like that. Your da—"

I held up a finger.

"Right. Come on." Lex glanced around. Spotted my cue case under a nearby chair. Pulled it out. Took the stick from me. Unscrewed the shaft from the butt, flipped the top open on the hard case, and slipped the sticks inside. Slinging the long case strap over his shoulder, he cupped my elbow.

I had stuck on the word *hospital,* rooted to the floor.

Absently, I'd reached for the ring hanging from the chain around my neck. At Lex's touch, I shook off my daze and dropped the ring.

"Where are you staying?" said Lex.

"Nowhere." My stomach squeezed. I allowed him to walk me to the door. "Motel on Thirty-Four."

"You're coming to my place." He glanced at me. "Don't worry, love. You can trust me."

"No, I can't." I could feel the tears forming. I swallowed hard. "I can't go home with you. I should talk to Dot."

"Let me go with you."

I shook my head. Before I could speak, a voice hollered from the rear of the hall. The shouting intensified. We turned. A young man jogged forward, followed by a small herd of beefy minions. The insults thrown in my direction did nothing to faze the other patrons. Nothing new for Jello's. Behind the bar, Jello called out, demanding payment of the young man's tab. Jello didn't care about fights as long as his end was covered.

"Did you take him?" whispered Lex. "Of course you did." He spun us back toward the door. Hurried our pace.

"Wasn't much of a hustle," I said. "He saw me beat the pants off his friend first. He's drunk."

"Drunk, stupid, and big. Not a good combination." Lex handed me the cue case.

"He practically begged me to—" The obscenity the guy shouted caught me off guard. "Vile boy. Guess he's worked himself into a lather about it at the bar. I am a mere female, you know. A blow to his pride. Took him three large before he gave up."

"Right. Blighter. He's going to catch us in the parking lot. Student, yes?"

Before the doors, Lex stopped. Pivoted. Retraced his steps toward the ape. Lex put out a hand as if to shake, then used it to steady the gorilla. "Hey, mate. Couldn't help but hear you. Let me correct the situation."

Behind him, the man's friends—an indistinguishable line of baseball hats, college-branded hoodies, and beards—blundered to a halt, confused by Lex's friendly voice and relaxed candor.

"What?" bellowed the man. He shook a fist in my direction. "Were you carrying her stick? She friggin' has her own cue? What the f—"

Lex cut off his drunken cursing. "Sorry, mate. Didn't catch your name. Drew, was it?"

"Yes, how—?"

"Your friend mentioned it." Lex jerked his chin toward the line of monkeys behind Drew. They shifted, widening the circle. One twisted away to wander back to the bar.

"Listen, Drew. She took you for a ride, did she? Are you upset that this young girl beat you in pool?" Lex's voice rose while seeming to drop. "You know, she's a brilliant mathematician. Really. It's all in the angles. Trajectories. That sort of thing. Her father's a professor. Maybe you had him. Physics. Genius, really. Doctor—"

"Williams?" offered Drew.

"You know him? You might know me as well."

"You're British."

"Accent gave it away, did it?" Lex smiled. "Yes, a doctoral student. I work for Williams. Unfortunate situation, his daughter." He gave a nod in my direction.

Leaning against the door, I shrugged. Gave Drew an apologetic smile.

"A bit touched. Explains the maths, yes? Can't help herself, you know what I mean?"

"What?" said Drew. "She seemed normal."

"We won't speak the words. Minor's right to privacy. So hard to tell sixteen from twenty-one these days."

Drew's eyes widened. "She's sixteen?"

"And Jello," Lex continued, "as all you students know, looks the other way on such things. Fake IDs and the lot. Probably why you and your friends are here. I trotted over to find her. Mission for Dr. Williams. Campus Police are on their way."

"Security? They're not cops."

"No, but they report criminal incidents to the police. Under the Clery Act, I believe. Campus police is not mall security, Drew. The actual police will be just behind them. Nothing they love more than a fake ID bust. Identity theft and the like is a serious concern these days."

As Drew swayed, Lex dropped an arm around his shoulder and steered him toward a table.

"Let's chat, Drew. Dr. Williams has a protocol for these things." Lex pulled out a chair.

Drew sank into it. His remaining friends drifted toward the pool tables.

Hovering above Drew, Lex crooked a finger at me and raised his voice. "Miss Williams, we need to settle this. If you could join us, please."

I slunk to their table, doing my best imitation of sixteen-going-on-twenty-something.

Lex cupped a hand around his mouth and raised his voice. "Jello, how much does he owe you?"

"Fifty," called Jello.

Drew blanched.

"Heavy night for three-dollar beer," said Lex. "All right, Drew. Let's pay Jello first. Jello only takes cash. Doesn't like to pay those pesky credit card service fees."

Or taxes, but I kept that thought to myself.

"Can't." Drew pointed at me. "She took all my money. I told Jello she'd have to pay."

"You lost your bet," I said. "Bets, rather. All six of them. After the first three times, you might have realized the odds were against you. Really, after losing the first two, it's sixty percent in favor of losing. A betting man should know these things."

"Miss Williams, what have we told you about speaking so bluntly? People perceive that as rude." Lex shook his head. "Sorry, Drew. Looks like I got here just in time."

He presented a clip of cash. Palmed the clip. Counted off what appeared to be fifty. Handed the folded notes to me. "Miss Williams, pay Jello. And tip him well."

I nodded meekly. Trotted to Jello and delivered the fold. "Payment for young Drew."

Jello scooped the bills into a meaty fist and dropped them in his till. "You're going to catch it one of these days, Fin."

"Not if they catch it first." I winked. "Drew had an extra Benjamin for you. Gratis. Also in case the others don't reconcile. These rich kids are the worst at paying their debts. Money spilling out of their pockets, yet too cheap to pay a tab."

"And too dumb not to see it fall out of their pockets and into your hands. I thought you went straight, hon."

"I did," I said. "Can I help it if these boys won't let themselves believe what's right in front of their eyes? If I don't hide my skill, it's not a hustle."

"This is Lex's money then?" Jello's smile stretched, making his chins wobble.

"I didn't say that. Lex would never short you, any more than I would. But Lex would rather have Drew pay his own bill. As he should." I leaned forward. "Jello, what did you hear about Penny Forbes dying?"

"Thought you knew, hon." Jello's chins quivered with a mournful shake. "Can't believe it. She was engaged, too, did you know that? Found a way up."

"Up?"

"Rich guy. Didn't surprise me too much. That Penny. Gorgeous and smart. A legend."

"Hold on." I checked on Lex. While drawing out a story with one hand, he slipped the money clip back into Drew's pocket. Typical Lex. Let Drew think he'd blown his cash when he woke hung over and broke.

I turned back to Jello. "Penny was engaged to a rich guy and OD'd on heroin? Doesn't add up, Jello. She didn't use and she'd never pimp out. She was a good roper, but never let herself get too dirty."

"I reckoned the same. After her momma—" His chins shook again.

"Exactly. The rich guy, was he a mark? Or legit?"

"Dunno, hon." Jello fixed his piggy eyes over my shoulder. "Lex is wrapping up."

I turned, catching the exuberant expression lighting Lex's face. He could be mistaken for a young doctoral student. A highlighted lock had fallen over his forehead. His lean physique gave the impression of slightness. I knew the wiry strength that hid beneath his designer button-down. He just needed a pair of wire-rims to complete the picture of a slightly nerdy but cute grad student. Not that Lex had ever set foot in a college class-room. No more than I had.

At least I didn't think so. You could never be sure with Lex.

I wouldn't put it past him to audit the classes that interested him. And it wouldn't surprise me if he had somehow obtained a diploma. He was good at that sort of thing. Got his kicks from pitting his wiles against bu-reaucratic quagmires. Anything that frustrated a normal person, Lex loved to unravel and beat.

Including trying to lure me back into his question-able operations. And other areas of his life.

Catching my eye, Lex gave me a slight nod. I slunk back to the table, seemingly chastened.

"Thanks for covering my tab," Drew said. "And if I see her in here again, I'll leave her alone."

"Do that, young man. Although I'd give Jello's a wide berth, if I were you. He overlooks anything but paying your bill, which you almost didn't do. But if you risk Jello's wrath and do see Miss Williams, give Mr. Jello the word that you've spotted this young sociopath. He'll escort her out the door. Likely you as well. Jello hates rats even more than scarpers. I think it's a cattle prod he uses."

Lex's smile quirked as he peered down his nose at me. "You heard that, Miss Williams? It's for your own good. Respectable young women don't hang out in pool halls."

I pursed my lips. Lex was really pushing it.

He grasped my elbow. "Past your bedtime, Miss Williams. Time to go home. Your father will be sorry to hear about this."

"He certainly would," I said dryly. My father was always sorry to hear about me and any sort of hustle—imagined or real. Particularly since my father was a cop.

And more crooked than any swindler I'd ever met.

"SEXY, SASSY, AND SOUTHERN SUSPENSE AT ITS BEST."

From *Wall Street Journal* bestselling author Larissa Reinhart, the first in the Southern con artist, romantic mystery thriller, the Finley Goodhart Crime Caper series. A 2021 Page Turner Awards winner.

SHE WANTS to use her criminal past to catch crooks. He wants her back. In the grift. And in his life. Can Finley Goodhart convince Lex that doing good is the greatest hustle of all?

"This is as fun a novel as it is moving and at times heartbreaking, never the more so when the final page comes and readers are only left wanting more."

Ex-grifter Finley Goodhart may try to stay on the straight and narrow, but walking that thin line becomes wobbly when she believes her friend Penny was murdered. The last thing she wants is to work with her ex-partner (and ex-boyfriend), the brilliant (brilliantly frustrating) British con artist, Lex Leopold. However, when it appears Penny's demise might be related to an exclusive matchmaking service for millionaires, Fin needs Lex's help to pull a long con to get the goods on Penny.

Romance is in the air for hustlers, gangsters, and their marks. Unfortunately for Fin and Lex, infiltrating the racket doesn't make for a match made in heaven. This Valentine swindle could stop their hearts for good.

LARISSA'S MYSTERY SERIES

15 MINUTES
16 MILLIMETERS
NC-17
A VIEW TO A CHILL
17.5 CARTRIDGES IN A PEAR TREE (novella)
18 CALIBER
18 1/2 DISGUISES
19 CRIMINALS
20 CARATS
21 GUNS

"Child star and hilarious hot mess Maizie Albright trades Hollywood for the backwoods of Georgia and pure delight ensues. Maizie's my new favorite escape from reality."

Ex-teen TV and reality star, Maizie Albright, returns home to Black Pine, Georgia, determined to start a new career as a private investigator, modeled after her childhood starring role as "Julie Pinkerton, Teen Detective." Unfortunately, Maizie's chosen mentor, Wyatt Nash of Nash Security Solutions, is not a willing teacher, and her learning curve includes becoming her own person after spending life under the thumb of managers, directors, and producers, particularly her stage-monster mother.

"Ms. Reinhart has struck gold with these characters and written them into a fabulous and funny mystery story. Twists and turns, romantic tension, great dialogue full of humor and fast quips, along with some Southern flair had these pages absolutely flying." — Great Escapes

"Readers who like a little small-town charm with their mysteries will enjoy Reinhart's series."

DENISE SWANSON, *NEW YORK TIMES*
BESTSELLING AUTHOR

A CHRISTMAS QUICK SKETCH (prequel)
PORTRAIT OF A DEAD GUY
STILL LIFE IN BRUNSWICK STEW
HIJACK IN ABSTRACT
THE VIGILANTE VIGNETTE
DEATH IN PERSPECTIVE
THE BODY IN THE LANDSCAPE
A VIEW TO A CHILL
A COMPOSITION IN MURDER
A MOTHERLODE OF TROUBLE

Meet Cherry Tucker, big in mouth, small in stature, and able to sketch a portrait faster than kudzu climbs telephone poles! The Cherry Tucker Mystery series (Henery Press) begins with Portrait of a Dead Guy, a 2012 Daphne du Maurier finalist, a 2012 The Emily finalist, a 2011 Dixie Kane Memorial winner, and a Woman's World Magazine book club pick for 2018!

"Reinhart manages to braid a complicated plot into a tight and funny tale. Cozy fans will love Cherry Tucker mysteries."

MARY MARKS, *NEW YORK JOURNAL OF BOOKS*

"As fun as it is moving and at times heartbreaking, never the more so when the final page comes and readers are only left wanting more."

CYNTHIA CHOW, *KING'S RIVER LIFE MAGAZINE*

THE PIG'N A POKE (free prequel, short story)
THE CUPID CAPER

Ex-con Finley Goodhart finds her criminal past — and criminal ex-boyfriend — useful in catching crooks. Can she make up for her past by helping victims double-cross their swindlers? More importantly, can she convince Lex that going straight is the best (and most challenging) hustle of all?

"Faced paced, bold, heartbreaking, this book has it all. Highly recommended for lovers of mystery and thrillers."

ABOUT THE AUTHOR

Wall Street Journal bestselling and international award-winning author Larissa Reinhart writes humorous mysteries and romantic comedies, including the critically acclaimed Maizie Albright Star Detective, Cherry Tucker Mystery, and Finley Goodhart Crime Caper series. Her works have been chosen as book club picks by *Woman's World Magazine* and *Hot Mystery Reviews*.

Larissa's family and dog, Biscuit, had been living in Japan, but once again call Georgia home. See them on HGTV's *House Hunters International* "Living for the Weekend in Nagoya" episode. Visit her website, LarissaReinhart.com, join her VIP Readers Group, and get a free short Finley Goodhart story.